BRIDGES

of

FLIGHT

before the

AMERICAN REVOLUTION

An Incredibly Dry Vintage Comedy

by

Kim Kacoroski

Cover art illustrations by Kim Kacoroski, Phillipe Velasquez, and Masha Tatarintsev

Visit the author website:
http://kimkacoroski.com

ISBN: 978-1-947036-09-3 (Paperback)

Version 2017.27.03

Book Five of Flight Series

and Book Six of Camelon Series

Bridges of Flight before the

American Revolution

Other Books in the Flight Series

Flight from Oblivion I

Eagle's Flight in the American Revolution II

Flight of the Ascendants in the American Revolution III

Choices from the American Revolution IV

Testimony V

Books in the Oblivion Series

Escape from Oblivion I

Beyond Oblivion II

Oblivion's Edge IV

Oblivion's Deal V

Flight from Oblivion VI

Books in the Camelon Series

The Promise of Camelon I

The Dragons of Camelon II

History of the World According to the Druids III

New Beginnings IV

The Kingdom of the Golden Tara V

Testimony VI

Chapter One

MOONSHINE

You came to me in a dream

Through a wispy autumn mist

And I followed you in the waving

Branches of a willow

There among the leaves we played

Under the cover of your intoxicating breath

Until the dawn changed into its early yellow

And in the morning's final hour

Armed with the embrace I craved

I awoke as you handed me a flower

Moonshine © Kim Kacoroski 1997

525 AD

IN A FIERY flash of lightning, a white-bearded horseman stormed into the quiet village of Garten, Ireland. Wearing a headdress of colored feathers, he quickly dismounted from his black stallion and opened his arms wide, greeting the crowd gathered around him. Quickly pulling a harp from his brilliant red bag, he plucked a few bold notes and sang to the townsfolk.

"It's Gemman the bard," Columba's mother mention in a low voice as she pushed him forward. "Get closer and sit beside your friends. You must hear what he has to say."

Awestruck by the dazzling display of ornaments and tapestries, the three-year-old boy hurried to join his companions in the front row. An older boy named Finnian reached for him and secured Columba in his lap. In a paternal manner, Finnian protected the young lad from horses' hooves and the roughhousing of larger playmates.

"Gemman is only three hundred and thirty-six years old," Finnian whispered to Columba. Nodding at the steed in the distance, he added, "Look, he brought a white Caspian horse from Persia."

Gemman put his harp aside and rolled out a carpet. Gingerly, he stepped onto the rug, which hovered a few inches above the ground. Making himself comfortable, Gemman relaxed as he sat down in the middle. The carpet rose another three feet higher in the air. Someone from the group handed Gemman a steaming cup of mead. The white-bearded man quieted and savored the beverage. He glanced at his horse standing nearby in a patch of grass. The Caspian mare flared her nostrils at the scented brew and snorted in discontent.

"Gemman took Arcas on a magic carpet ride," another boy commented to Finnian in a hushed voice.

Without responding, Columba recalled the story about how Arcas had pulled the sword from the stone and became leader of the varied population in northwestern Europe. After thwarting the alien agenda to conquer the planet, Arcas died while defending the Castle Marlboro from Roman clergy. The carpet ride served to bridge the celestial realm with the earth-bound engagements.

Arcas's granddaughter married an Irish chieftain, the cousin of Columba's mother. Free from the Roman legions, the granddaughter ran operations at the Hill of Tara, an outpost in Ireland. People called the granddaughter, Tinka. She worked with Lady Casper, the mother of Arcas's father. For seven hundred years, Lady Casper continued the mission of the Goblecki-Tepe civilization at a smaller site along the Caspian Sea, Tepe Giyan. Stewards cared for the Caspian horses under the guidance of Lady Casper. Having successfully survived the demise of Gondwanaland, the horses kept the spirit of the planet alive as Roman legions ravaged the terrain with their chariots.

Tepe Giyan served as an extension of the Iron Mountain network, which existed long before Eden or Atlantis. A group of intergalactic hostages attained freedom by using their talents to create the MidEarth. home of the spirits emerging as caretakers for the planet. After Lilith poisoned the Gondwanaland civilization, a legion from Iron Mountain took a cutting from the Tree of Life. They immigrated to another landmass and propagated the offshoot in present-day North Korea. After the destruction of planet Mu, the refugees formed another civilization called Lemuria. Working with a collection of nature devas, the Lemurians salvaged the Eden prototypes. They developed strains resistant to Serpentine poisoning or infiltration, which could guide human evolution. After the Titan Atlas founded Atlantis, some inhabitants with the Gaud DNA formed powerful connections with those who had destroyed Planet Mu. They captured and enslaved Lemurians to build energetic vortexes and produce the pyramid civilizations. Celestials landed on the planet to support the human family. Metatron, an ascended group of humans, obtained the designs of a powerful intergalactic fortress from the god, Mercury. Metatron's group connected with the rebellion instigated by a wife of Rameses II. The group gave them a translation of Metatron's Cube in the shape of a icosahedron. The natives fashioned green-emerald balls in this shape for their peace of mind. The shift in mental attitude proved successful as they freed their souls and overthrew their oppressors.

The mare from Tepe Giyan deliberately walked away from the group unattended and grazed in the distant meadow. A surviving female spirit from the ancient civilization of Gondwanaland, the Caspian horse stunned onlookers with her divine beauty. With the music ringing in his ears, Columba watched the animal move gracefully past the throng. Gemman smiled at his audience, mesmerized by his treasure. He sang of a timeless place known as Iona, an island in the Scottish Hebrides. Like a thousand twinkling bells, the bright melody filled the air with complexities that stretched the consciousness of the listeners. Gemman's lyrics continued for hours and told the story of how Egyptian priests consecrated Iona in 2400 BC. After defeating the Lord of the Rings, the MidEarth sought to restore the planet. The rings referred to the sheets of ice encircling the globe. The devastation wrought by the intergalactic wars created these rings. The oceans splashed so high into the atmosphere that the water froze.

"You must go to Iona," he said in a lullaby to Columba. Looking directly at the small boy, Gemman emphasized his request with a twinkle in his eye. Dazed by the spectacle, Columba nodded his response before dozing off. His mother came and carried him away. After tucking him in his bed, she left him as he slept.

Columba dreamed of the royal necropolis in ancient Egypt. Called the District of the Poker Tree, the inhabitants gambled with the Tree of Life or Kabhala. Druid priests stole offshoots and planted them throughout present-day Europe. Eventually, the priest's common ash became known as *Fraxinus excelsior* by the stray Roman legions heralding its life-giving properties. Roman clergy members sought to reverse its effect by burning the tree and anointing natives with the adage, *ashes to ashes; dust to dust*. The natives saw through the ruse, choosing the philosophy to avoid death. They escaped by peering through the holes in thought, and referred to the imposed ceremonies as *holy*.

In his dream, several priests with ankh crowns stood around a small tree. One shoveled while the others watched for intruders. Freeing the ash tree from the sandy loam, they raced out of the Egyptian compound before the guards woke from their induced slumber. The man with the shovel hid the tree in the folds of his brown robe, which kept him warm in the cold desert night. Another priest took the shovel and tossed it to an Egyptian Queen, the wife of the pharaoh. Climbing a ladder, they scurried up the clay wall of the garden. On the other side, the priests jumped on a series of tiled roofs and stealthily made their way to a cobblestone ally. Tied to a bush behind a stable, their steeds waited nervously in the foreign land. The priest dunked the tree in a nearby watering bough before wrapping it in straw from the bin. He covered the ash with a papyrus mat, securing the contents and disguising the tree as a roll of parchment.

An Egyptian Prince led the mounted men to the closest gate, where he instructed his soldiers to open it for the company. The priests fled the city and rode three hours to a well on the outskirts of the oasis. Smoke filled the air, hiding the well in the mists of a dark night. The vapor-covered bodies of the winged dragons sauntering around the well.

"Outta here," a dragon whispered before spreading his wings.

The priest with the ash tree hopped onboard and grasped the robe of the rider in front. Later the next morning, they landed in a Gaul encampment known as Silvanectii. A blue-robed sylvan took the wrapped ash from the priest and assumed care of the plant. The dragons flew to their caves in the hillside as the crowned priests met with the sylvans. Fires from openings in the warm burrows filled the air with exotic scents. Famished by their journey, they delightedly partook of the feast waiting for them inside the earthen domains.

"We'll wait until this offshoot of the Tree of Life matures and then plant an offshoot in Gilgamesh's gardens."

Located in present-day Versailles, Gilgamesh's gardens rivaled the Lemurian collection, which had been destroyed during the intergalactic wars. The Nile River parted temporarily as fifty percent of Lemurian sank. This released the Hebrews to the deserts, where they wandered aimlessly until Gilgamesh's cousin appropriated another settlement for them. By the time Moses realized that he had been duped by those initiating the attack on Lemuria, aliens had killed off all the Egyptians. Scrapping their experimental results underneath the pyramids, the invaders resumed the Atlantean genetic modifications. They found new pharaohs to replace the slain ones, preserved and catalogued underneath the stone monuments for future reference. Crawling out of the ashes of the previous Egyptian culture, the order of the phoenix emerged and established a pyramidal money scheme known as the Phoenicians. Though successful in overthrowing their Serpentine oppressors, they succumbed to the jaws of the Sea People. Lemurian refugees intermarried with Atlantean survivors called the Celtics. In collaboration, they formed the Sea People and Druids.

Columba awoke, slightly startled by the information conveyed in his dreams. Leaving his pile of bedstraw, he wandered outside of the wooden shack. Perched on his magic carpet, he found Gemman talking to the elders around a dying fire. The embers glowed in the dark night and lit the features on the faces of those assembled. Spotting his father at the campground, Colomba hurried toward him. His father scooped him up in his arms and held him close against the warmth of his chest.

Wide-eyed, Columba turned and stared at the group from the comfort of his father's embrace.

"In Iona, we have a sacred heart," Gemman explained. "The Serpentine priests removed the hearts of those in the pyramid civilizations."

Colomba's father covered the boy's ears with his large palm. Colomba blinked at Gemman.

"We recovered the heart from the body of the mutant merman and gave it a proper burial, one befitting a king," Gemman told those gathered around him. "The Roman occultists will never think to look where we buried it."

Colomba squirmed and his father placed him solidly on the ground. The boy stared quizzically at the face of Gemman. Kneeling over the ground, Columba drew a valentine in the dirt. Gemman peered over the rim of his risen carpet at the design. Without any hesitation, the bard continued with his tales, recounting the Gauds contribution to European history.

"When Zeus teamed up with the maddening crowd from Aldebaran to raze the settlements of Europa, he established another monetary system. Some, like the Cathars, will claim that Sin or Ishtar birthed the planet, but those from Iron Mountain have another story. The Greeks know Sin as Persephone. Hired by the Kings of Pleiades, she provided them with seven daughters, who protected the souls of Gondwanaland. The blame for the demise of the post-Eden civilization goes to the heavenly bull of Aldebaran. Aldebaran attacked the

Pleiades with funds collected by Lilith's descendants. Gondwanaland became divided over the money, which almost annihilated the Tree of Life."

Taking a deep breath, Gemman resumed his narration as Columba drew flowers around his heart in the sand. "Luckily, the spiritual warriors of the times were also highly skilled horticulturists. Propagation of the Tree of Life occurred throughout history of the world, at least according to the Druids."

Wide awake with the words of Gemman echoing in the camp, Columba rose from his sketch and began gathering sticks and stones for adding another dimension to the flat artwork. His father watched him wander from the crowd, and glanced at the shadows in the nearby woods. The white Caspian horse stood at the edge of the groove. She shook her head and whinnied softly, welcoming the boy near her. Intent on his endeavors, Columba briefly looked up at the mare before reaching for a shiny stone in the dirt.

Cradling his collection in his arms, Columba returned to his lines in the sand. The tension in his father's shoulders relaxed as his son played quietly by his feet. Careful to avoid stepping on the design, Columba's father questioned Gemman as the poet paused to sip his mead. "So what are we going to do about the sacred heart?"

"Well, that's another story," Gemman replied, gazing softly at Columba's valentine.

Chapter Two

AFTER GEMMAN DECIDED to go to bed, Columba took his father's hand and walked back to his pile of bedstraw. He blinked at the darkness and listened to the familiar sounds of the nearby woods. Falling asleep within minutes, Columba lapsed into another dream. Back at the sylvan camp, he dined with the others as a young, adult male. Wearing leggings and a blue tunic, he matched the sylvan hosts. A few women in blue dresses sat with the men at the table and discussed the findings of the Alemanni, the male counterpart of Avalon. They expected the Alemanni by dawn. As an adult, Columba lingered in the room and overheard several stories. One of the discourses captivated him.

A Druid priest told him about the experience in the District of the Poker Tree, the place where souls bind to eternity instead of life. After the bullish squadron of Aldebaran razed the European terrain, Zeus and his followers began experimenting in the Minoan region. With the help of Sauron and other crazed geneticists, they created a monster called a minotaur. The Minoans employed the Phoenicians to sell their pottery and the bullish monster came with the enterprise. Whoever didn't comply with the trade became trapped in a labyrinth with the minotaur. After a hundred years, the minotaur labyrinth became multidimensional. Presently, the free-trade association worked with the sole surviving Gaud, Diana, to establish a base in Greece. In a couple thousand years, they expected to be powerful enough to defeat the minotaur in the economic labyrinth. Those living near the District of the Poker Tree look forward to the day when they could smash their surplus pots.

Columba awoke early the next morning to the sounds of laughter and lighthearted chatter. He hurried out of his bedroll to join the celebration. The scent of cooked meats and spiced broths lent a sense of heartiness to the dewy morning vapors. The white Caspian horse remained distant from the festivities at the edge of the woods, while Gemman plucked a few chords from his harp. After grabbing a bowl full of stew, Columba sat down with a group of children. Eager to hear Gemman's next song, they squeezed together in various nooks and tree limbs. Noting their rapt attention, Gemman grinned and began singing.

As the lyrics of the tune hung in the air, Columba imagined himself as a sylvan greeting the rugged Alemanni. One of the men approached him and slipped an emerald inside his hand. Leaning close, he said in a low voice, "This is for peace of mind." After gently patting his shoulder, the Alemanni joined the serious discussion at the far end of the room.

Glancing at the object in his hands, the sylvan left the domain. He went to the closest stream and washed the icosahedron crystal until it opened like a mediative lotus. The emerald crystal held the records of the intergalactic pentagon. As he visualized the five-sided structure surrounding the three kings from different realms of the galaxy, another story entered his thoughts. He visualized a floating airship carrying celestials from various enlightened civilizations dimensions away. They landed near a rock found hundreds of miles to the northeast, near the origins of King Arthur's maternal grandmother. When nephilim ambushed the third group of intergalactic pilgrims, a grandchild of Adam and Eve seized control of the airship and sought refuge in the heavens. A messenger of the Gauds with winged sandals presented the escapee with a cube containing encapsulated information. The emerald crystal in his possession represented a section of the cube, which the messenger had handed the ascended grandchild. Dubbed Metatron by the Gauds, the grandchild joined forces with the others working with the celestials, who settled on the earth.

Columba became conscious of his present surroundings as the visualization drifted away with the chords from Gemman's sparkling music. Instead of staying with the rest, he rose and scurried over to the river. Several river stones glistened in a slow-moving eddy. Without entering the water, Columba picked up one of the smooth, polished rocks and held it in his dominant right hand. He skipped it over the current moving swiftly in the distance. Finding another stone, he threw it over the water and watched it bounced across the waves. Another stone captivated him and he pried it from the river bed without getting wet. Stopping for a moment to examine the rock as it reflected a fiery streak of sunlight, he put in pocket of his tunic and climbed the bank to rejoin the camp.

Never overstaying his welcome, Gemman left the village as quickly as he had entered. Columba lingered on the edge of the thicket with his stone in one hand. He waved to Gemman as he rode his steed out of camp. The Caspian mare trail behind several steps and whinnied at Columba as she passed. Hearing the sound, Columba stared in amazement at the horse. The simple acknowledgement of his presence stunned the small boy. He stood silently and watched the parade head down the road.

Columba headed back to his shack. Greeted at the threshold by an older brother, the lad opened the palm of his hand and revealed the river stone. The older boy noticed the rock ceremoniously displayed in the tiny hand. Stepping back a few feet from the demonstration, he carefully considered weight of the prized object. Without calling attention to the find, he asked with a hint of caution, "What did you find at the river?"

Removing the shiny stone from view, Columba pocketed in the folds of his tunic and proudly stated as if tested by an instructor, "Peace of mind."

Without hesitation Columba brushed past his brother and raced to the confines of his sleeping quarters. He extracted a small box from a cubby near his mat. Lifting the lid of the wooden container, he deposited the rock with the treasured collection. When a sylvan passed through the village ten years later, Columba accepted the emerald crystal from his opened hand. Adding it to his collection near his bedstraw, Columba packed the box in his knapsack and headed for the Hebrides.

There, he founded a shelter for refugees from the mainland. He buried the Celtic warriors from Tara there, while accepting soldiers from the Druid Isles and Dragon flyers from Scotland. Calling the established site, Iona, he networked with those at an Egyptian well, one haunted by the half-sister of King Arthur. White-eared dragons carried the emerald through the skies to the oasis, where a priest embedded the stone in a golden crown. Sizing the crown to fit the head of a female statue, he dedicated the artwork to the divine feminine. Known as Ma Ray, the energy conceived the planet as place of hope and refuge.

Vikings sacked the settlement at Iona, and crucified one of the soldiers from the House of Brus in Scotland. They carved out his heart in the same manner as the Serpentines had done to those imprisoned at the pyramid civilizations. Through trade routes, the programmed minions from the Gray's base at Iceland brought the heart to Solomon's temple. They restored the occult headquarters in Jerusalem and reinterred a section of the counter-pentagon, called the Pentarch. Practicing the rituals of Isis, the severed hearts corresponded to the replacement of the crystal skulls with victimized skulls and bones. Through trades with the Turks inhabiting Constantinople, the Ma Ray statue made its way to a compound, one used by the orthodox priests in the area. In this manner, the cults attempted to resurrect the Gauds they worshipped from the intergalactic wars. The ruse succeeded in creating an illusion enveloping the planet in darkness.

Descendants of Merlin, the House of Brus came from Denmark. The successor of Mab, Queen of the Fairies, took mercy on Columba and his warriors and carried their souls to the MidEarth. After the fall of Glastonbury Abbey, Merlin fled to the MidEarth. Mab joined the archangels overseas on the American continents, as the new Fairy Queen Titania sought Merlin's help. He entered the dream state of his descendants, who had intermarried with the dwarves, and urged them to fight with Gandolf, another wizard in Norway.

With aid from the fairy kingdom, they pushed the Vikings out of Scandinavia. The Vikings worked with the Serpentine descendants of the Emperor Claudius, forming an allegiance with the nephilim, progeny of Gilgamesh. An international slave trade culminated in the First Crusade. The trade began with Rollo, who assumed control of operations pertaining to England, Sicily, Arabia, and Antioch. The Viking pirate, Harold the FairHair, mentored Rollo's father and established a kingdom near Iona. Having found Iona eerily vacated by the time of their arrival, the fleeing Viking armies sought comforts elsewhere. Eventually, the House of Brus ambushed them in Normandy. They established Norman the Conqueror to retake the Viking outposts as the son of Robert the Magnificent. Rollo escaped to Sicily and sold his soul to Sauron, an evil wizard from the dark days of Atlantis before its collapse. Working with the Roman Empire to displace the Atlantean survivors stationed at the Hill of Tara in Ireland, he persecuted Columba's Celtic ancestors from the O'Neill tribe. He stole Columba's crest and brought it to Sauron, who networked with Armenia to establish the slave trade. Sauron's counterpart in France, Germaine managed a Chateau. Norman's son, Henry I, attacked the Germaine Chateau. Rollo's son, Robert Curthose defeated Henry I and seized the coat of arms from the House of Brus. His son, Henry II, escaped and enlisted Eleanor of Aquitaine, who needed support as well. Setting up a new base, they were eventually taken over by Germaine's minions from the Priory of Scion. Lost in a dream-state wrought by illusionists, the couple began placing progeny from the Henry line in Druid settlements established across the Atlantic Ocean. The granddaughter of Eleanor by the King of France, bore the same name as her mother, Marie de Champagne. While her mother ran with the Alemanni, Marie remained in Eleanor's court. The leader of the Alemanni carried on the work of Avalon from the Spencer's line. Outsiders called him *Robin* for the bird with the red breast that brought hope and renewal. After his father's death, Robin frequented the local abbey, where he earned the nickname Hood for the mantle covering his head. Far more livelier than the heartless escapades of Eleanor, Robin Hood developed a reputation balancing the scales of justice as well as a fondness for Marie's mother, otherwise known as the Maid Marian. As Eleanor became engrossed in the antics of her sons by Henry II, Marie supplied them with information.

Chapter Three

YOUNG HENRY II RODE toward Eleanor, his newly wedded wife. Mounted on his favorite steed, he approached her without slowing down to hear her latest insult. Rather than listen, he roared his latest request, "Quit brooding over your losses in France and get ready to come to England with me."

Glancing at the new King of England, Eleanor quieted and swallowed hard. She ignored his booming voice and focused on a red rose growing in the garden. Eleanor extended one arm and cradled the flushed blossom in her hand. Without looking up, she commented, "The pope granted you one annulment in exchange for the Tara in Ireland. He won't protect you in England."

"Stephen lost both to the pope and the Priory of Scion."

Eleanor plucked the rose off the bush and turned to face Henry II. "You were born in France and you'll die in France."

"That's not my fault," he retorted, finally calming his horse. The animal lowered its head and began to feed on the grass. Henry leaned over the saddle and peered at Eleanor. "My maternal grandfather bound me to the Gray-Norman-Vikings." Straightening in his position, he eyed Eleanor carefully as he rhetorically quizzed, "What do Normans do?" He picked up the reins of the feeding stallion and together they walked away with his answer. "They invade."

"They killed my granddaughter," Eleanor retorted.

Henry's horse stopped in its tracks. With a nod to one shoulder, he replied, "Never name a daughter, Scholastique, while living under Serpentine-Salish law. You knew that."

Eleanor threw the red rose against the ground. She screamed at Henry, "You're my cousin. Our common ancestor Spartacus bonds us."

Henry dismounted and walked over to Eleanor. The remembrance of Sparatus's uprising relaxed the tension in his demeanor. A descendant of Prometheus's daughter from Andromeda, Spartacus led Gallia Aquitania against Zeus's eagle. With help from several archangels from Angles, Germany, the Gauls destroyed Zeus's earthbound incarnation. Picking up the red rose, he gently handed it over to her.

"Ever since the Romans crucified Spartacus, the Roman Serpentines have called us *pagi* or pagans. Then they made us *civitates* and civilized the Atlantean-Celtic survivors. To participate in their affairs and earn the right to vote, we must suffer. *Suffrage* is their program, lest we break the Gaud-spell, which serves as their gospel."

The Gauds sponsored the immigration of refugees from the planets that they obliterated. Through rape and torture, their genetic code made its way into the human form. Diana, the Gaud of the hunt, refused to collaborate. With the aid of Prometheus and the Titans, they forged a settlement called Atlantis, anticipating the destruction of

Lemuria. Lemuria existed to work with the evolutionary patterns of planetary light forms. After Lemuria collapsed under heavy fire during the intergalactic wars, Atlantis carried on the work. Hades infiltrated Atlantis and began genetically modifying the code in secret. When Atlantis sank, survivors fled to different regions. Unfortunately, those attempting to destroy the genetic codes found shelter at Mount Athos, which maintained communications with Mount Olympus. With the help of Hades, a group of Dragon flyers failed to evolve during the intergalactic wars of ancient Egypt. Remaining stuck in a paradigm concerning Apollo the Sun Gaud, they formed their own court and adopted Constantine as their own. Their minions sacrificed millions to complete the transition.

With an air of resignation, Eleanor accepted the flower from his hands. Henry softly kissed her forehead. She wrapped her arms around his midriff and held him tight.

Henry looked into her eyes. "Did you and Louis ever think that you would get away with creating Oedessa County for Spartacus's tribes?"

She turned aside and stared at the ground. "Yes, we failed in the eyes of Rome. We are not caesars, or ever meant to be. You know that."

"I do. The Romans must hide the ages of the women, which they try to civilize." He sighed, before continuing, "In the case of Marie's friend, they will invent an entire new life for her. They might even make Scholastique her daughter."

"After they killed Robin Hood's younger sister, Scholastique, we knew that we had to run to England," Eleanor replied, decisively wringing her free hand. Waving him away, she composed herself. "Off you go, Henry. Robin can help you there."

"I'll need him to keep our sons in line," he speculated.

"Yes, I know," she said ruefully. "That is the Roman family."

"Like snakes, they eat each other."

"Stay away, Henry, or else I will kill you."

His stallion gathered speed as Henry grinned. "I will make you my prisoner."

"I shall be safer that way," she observed. "Bye, my love. I will visit you in England, after I make plans with my seer."

Two days following Henry's departure, Eleanor and Marie journeyed to a group of Dragon flyers stationed in the local Pyrenees Mountains. They entered the tent of Eleanor's favorite seer from the Indus Valley. Sitting down, the mother-daughter team asked the gypsy about how to get-along with Henry II.

Without a word, the woman overturned a tarot card and placed it upright on the green scarf between them. Eleanor reached for the card and studied it. Developed by Atlantean refugees with runaway artists from Andromeda, the tarot spread inspired creative thinking about the challenges of the times. For this reason, the Romans discouraged the use.

"Henry is on a slippery slope," the woman remarked.

"We know that," Marie said dryly.

"He's better off in England," the woman added as she unflipped the next card.

Eleanor placed the first card down to compare it to the second. "It's the chariot-reversed. Looks like those ego-driven maniacs from Rome have plans to tame Connecticut, the O'Connor land mass."

"Eventually the newly formed Columbus company will name it for one of their bankers, someone called America. He'll map the operation out for them."

"I suggest taking the advice of a war-vet of the Crusades called Francis. His father named him for the Frank's Salish operations, but he defected. Working with the raped refugees, he developed a code called the Serenity Prayer. We deciphered the code. It advised us to stay balanced as the Romans attempt to run us over, literally."

"Yes, they took our wheels for their chariots," Marie complained. "Now they want to make roads, where we prefer the off-beaten trails and enjoy our moments of solitude and discovery."

"Yes, it looks like Connecticut is about to be discovered, give or take a few hundred years."

"Now what do we do?" Eleanor questioned.

"Stay serene," the reader advised. "By the looks of the next card, it is time to get the angels in on the action. Tell Michael to modify the recipe for Chalice Well to take to the imprisoned natives at the place the Latin pirates call *open door*."

"Oh, Puerto Rico!" Marie exclaimed.

Eleanor glanced at her. "How do you know?"

"A Robin told me," she whispered. "He runs with the Welsh Dragon flyers. Like Henry, the Columbus company is grooming them for their pirating operations. With enough work, they will eventually have a Manchurian candidate known as Drake, which the Latin pirates will claim as their own dragon or *draco*."

Eleanor rose and steadied herself on her bare feet. "I got it. Come on, Marie, there is no time to loose."

Marie stood and nodded to the gypsy. "Thanks for the heads up on the upcoming war between angels and demons."

Remaining seated, the woman looked at the ground and mused, "Gallia Aquitania will be called Basque country in a few hundred years."

Eleanor climbed to a cave on the other side of two openings in the cliff towering overhead. "Oh, Michael, we need your assistance. Just take your platform over to Connecticut and give the prisoners water from Chalice Well."

"That's a great idea!" the archangel shouted with hearty zest. "That should free them up and they can ride with me across the sea. We'll give the recipe to the refugees from Spica located on the east coast."

"The Columbus company will call them *Indians* and connect them with the Silk Road," Marie interjected.

Eleanor studied Marie closely. She decided, "Go play with Robin. I'll send a note to Henry about the change in plans. You can take it with you."

Months later, Marie handed the note over to Henry while he knelt in prayer at an English abbey. Without removing her veil, she prayed as he read Eleanor's letter. Concealing his smirk under the watchful eyes of nearby monks, Henry responded in a hushed voice, "Mother Superior (Eleanor) has interceded, again." With a wave of his hand, he serenely said, "Run along my child."

Marie glared at him, before making the sign of the cross in front of her face for all the saints to see. She hurried over to Robin's groove located on the other side of town. Finding the encampment vacant, she helped herself to a bowl of soup from a pot left hanging over the dying fire. A small boy appeared from behind a tree. Wearing a clean, bright-blue tunic, he joined her by the campfire.

"Who are you?" Marie asked.

He sipped water from his canteen and nonchalantly said, "I don't know. The sylvans picked me up. They told me that I came from over there." The youth pointed to a dense cloud of smoke hanging over the forest to the east.

"I don't think that you should go back," Marie observed.

"Me neither. It stinks," he said, wrinkling his nose in disgust."

Robin returned with his group of merry men and sat down beside Marie. "Who is this wood nymph?"

Shaking her head in disbelief, Marie covered her face to feign embarrassment. She did not answer Robin's question. Calmly reclining on the ground's slope, he pretended to ignore Marie's reaction. The boy grinned at their antics.

"I'm not a wood nymph. I'm a sylvan," he claimed proudly. The boy pointed to several small figures hiding in the underbrush.

Robin glanced in their direction and nodded at the boy. "Oh yes, I see. The wood elves picked you up. You are obviously not a wood nymph." Turning to the sylvans for further information, he watched them motion the boy away. "You arrived fully clothed into this world."

The boy smiled at Robin with an emphasized nod.

"Well, you are one of us. Your name must be Sylvan." Staying by Marie's side, Robin instructed, "Get something to eat. Then you can go play with the elves. You must fend for yourself and take care of yourself."

The boy quietly obeyed, before heading back into forest.

"He's a smart lad," Marie remarked as she watched the elves lead him back into the forested density. "He'll be safe there."

Chapter Four

A HALF YEAR later, Henry II took Sylvan with him on an escapade in Leinster, Ireland. Barely three years of age, Sylvan had reached manhood by the standards of the dragon-flyer community. They entered a monastery and found several nuns and priests waiting for them behind the sacristy. An elderly woman dressed in the black robes of a nun, rose from her chair to greet them.

"I'm the daughter of the late King Dewi of Wales," she said, offering Henry a piece of bread and goblet of wine. "My name is Crierwy. Today, I represent the universe. The high kings of Ireland are concerned that the monsters created by the Atlantean infiltrators on Mount Athos will take over Ireland."

Sylvan accepted read and wine from the nun, before climbing into a nearby chair. He watched the interaction silently from his perch. Henry pulled some cheese out of his knapsack and shared it with the others.

One nun interjected, "We heard about Great Balls of Fire in the Mideast. Joslin, King Arthur's sister, put the genetic mistake out of its misery."

"Someday, they will call them dinosaurs," another added.

"These are smaller and more human-like. They carry the Serpentine code," a priest reported. "They lack the ability to think in universal terms and don't play well with others."

"I see," Henry said, rubbing his head. Looking directly at Criewry, he asked, "What do you suggest?"

"Use the water from Chalice Well to genetically restore the soul. Though it is like working backwards, I think that we can spike the holy water."

"Didn't we already do that?" a monk asked.

"Not to address this issue. If the monsters come over here, we'll make them go to church and baptize them," a nun answered.

"Excellent idea. Then we'll tell them to avoid sex, so that they can't propagate, at least not as fast," another monk added.

Henry II squirmed in his seat and looked at Sylvan. "There's one more detail. The Serpentines intend to fortify their position in the Pentarch, which replaced our intergalactic pentagon. I can sow the seeds of disillusion in the face of the evil wizards controlling the Pentarch. These illusionists operate the Silk Road from the Serpentine's base in ancient Scythia."

"A code for planetary destruction has been seeded in the human line of Tumbinai Setsen," a monk confessed. "A representative of the Powrs Kingdom told me. He goes by Roderick, but maintains a low profile because his legal documents have been altered to escape notice by the Roman Empire. Tumbinai is their programmed candidate to dominate the Silk Road. His son will be the human equivalent of Great Balls, quite a monster."

After the meeting, Sylan stayed and rode with Crierwy to Chalice Well. Still small in stature, he easily fitted in the saddle on the back of Crierwy's dragon. Named Elissa, the golden Sea Dragon queen, soared high in the starry skies. Sylvan watched the world below as they drifted between airy clouds back to England. After collecting water from the well, they carried flasks to the four directions. First, they landed in Japan. Several of the samurai emerged from a concealed temple in a mountain forest to greet them.

"We foresaw this flask in a dream," a monk told her. Then he rushed to store the vessel in a safe place.

The other monks waved her off as they left for the next site. Descending in one of the art forms of the Nazca lines, they reached the southern hemisphere by nightfall. Elissa headed straight for the eye of the lizard, where a Pantagon accepted the water.

"When I heard about the mission, I left Pantagonia for the lizard," the gentle giant told them with a smile. Hurrying away with the water, he never bothered to wave good-bye.

The next day, they reached the third site inhabited by Eskimos. Gathered around a large whale, they dropped their activities for the water. A man wearing a fur parka told them, "The whale directed us here and told us to look for water."

Taking the flask from Criewry's hands, he rushed to store it near the warm body of the whale. The others waved as Elissa carried

Criewry and Sylvan away to the next location. Instead of returning to England, they passed through another dimension and brought the last batch to Iona.

At Iona, Sylvan scurried down Elissa's shiny gold scales and wandered toward the desolate dunes. Glancing at the sea's horizon, he saw the forms of the merpeople in the distance. For a moment, he waited and studied the sand beneath his feet as sensed their message. They invited him inside the abbey ruins, where an ancient library held information on the intergalactic pentagon destroyed by aliens.

Criewry joined Sylvan on the beach. Standing beside him briefly, she quietly mentioned, "I can help you find the information on Metratron's Cube. Let's go find that library."

"Metatron?" Sylvan questioned, raising his head.

"The Gaud's messenger, Mercury, gave the ascended artists the data. Though the stellar fortress collapsed under pressure, Henry II claims that it is worth recovering."

"We can make some adjustments," Sylvan said as he followed Criewry inside the abbey ruins.

A priest emerged from the shack located on the outskirts of the perimeter. Folding his arms inside the sleeves of his cloak, he greeted them, "I heard about your mission through the Horsetail communication network. Here are the notes on Metratron's work." He handed Sylvan a scroll as he slightly bowed his head in reverence. "This is a sacred place in the world."

Sylvan unrolled the document and examined the contents. "Great, it's in pictures that I can read."

As Sylvan sat down on the freshly swept tiles lining the floor of the roofless room, the priest explained about how Iona survived the conquest of Henry II's sponsors. After the Romans crucified the insurrection in Jerusalem, Joseph of Arimathea recovered the seven bodies and embalmed them according to the ancient Egyptian rites. His group fled to the Alemanni station for immediate protection, before making his way to Egypt. The bodies floated across the Nile River as the Anks had done. This gave them spiritual immunity from the occultists masterminding Rome from Narni.

"Who is the present Queen of Avalon," Criewry asked, changing the subject.

"After Scholastique's murder, the job went to Gemma's granddaughter by the name of Rousseau. Rousseau is a word for red hair, which is what happens with dragon-flyer training."

"Sounds like a seasoned warrior," Criewry remarked.

"Yes, the hair color becomes difficult to alter," the priest admitted as he rubbed his shaved head.

"Beats going gray."

"Literally," Sylvan interjected. Standing upright, he pulled a stone lodged in a crevice of a crumbling wall. "Why do they say that Jesse's heart is here?"

Without a word, Criewry gently took his chubby hand and led him to a courtyard. She pointed to the names suddenly appearing on the broken wall in front of them. Clutching the stone in one hand, Sylvan fingered the writing. Awestruck, he dropped her hand and replaced it with the stone.

"They buried Jesse's wife and his adopted mother here," the priest told them. "Scholastique is here too."

"Did Jesse's wife have red hair?" Sylvan asked, gazing at the priest.

"Yes. Miriam adopted Jesse, after the Lady of the Lake placed her child with Joseph."

"Miriam was Joseph's daughter?" he questioned.

"Yes," he said with a sigh. "She was a relation of King Arthur." Looking around the confines, the priest admitted, "These foundations contain secrets that most do not want to believe. Otherwise, they would have to quit denying the ongoing genetic experimentation of the dark wizards. They would have to get over the trauma of losing both Atlantis and Lemuria." Wrenching his hands inside the folds of his robes, he added, "Meanwhile, a daughter of Henry II and Eleanor must bear the cross of the New Jerusalem, which is like a new world order for the traffickers."

"Another is intended for Antioch," Creirwy commented. "It's all for the sake of marketing. After beheading him, they took the brains of John the Baptist to Mount Athos. Olympus wanted them."

His hands left the folds of his coat, and he relaxed. Leaning against a fallen pillar, the priest supported his weight with a bared, extended arm. "The alien network from the Germaine Chateau in France intends to line the routes with convents of their sacred hearts. It is a way of programming women for another form of slavery."

"Nothing is sacred," Sylvan murmured.

"It is all a question of values," Crierwy responded, removing a container of water from her knapsack. "We don't value monsters, so we came here to stop the trafficking."

With a polite nod, the priest accepted the flask from Criewry. He said, "Those work with the Silk Road usually develop stigmatas as a form of protection. The wounds bleed when you are getting too involved. Unless you are a dealer, everyone gets crucified on the route in some way or another. It can be disastrous for empaths."

With a wink, she motioned Sylvan toward the exit. He hopped and skipped outside the abbey ruins. Elissa waited patiently for them near a hidden stash of dragon meal.

"I value trees," Sylvan announced as he slid into his saddle.

Strapping him in tightly, the priest smiled. "Spoken like a true Druid." Patting Elissa affectionately on the snout, he advised, "Weather the tides of life by flying with dragons."

Chapter Five

CRIERWY LEFT SYLVAN near Robin's encampment and hurried back to Wales. Landing in a small clearing, Elissa snorted more smoke in the air to disguise their departure as Sylvan politely waved goodbye. Several elves ran to him from the forest and ushered Sylvan to a hiding place within the underbrush.

"Shhh," they instructed in a whisper. "The sheriff is out trafficking stray children."

Sylvan remained quiet and peered through the dense underbrush. Accepting his present circumstances, he longed for his former freedom with Elissa and Crierwy.

"Ok, we can move now," the head elf told the others. He paused for a moment and noticed Sylvan wiping a tear from his eye. Turning his head, he informed his companions, "We lost him."

When Sylvan overheard his words, he sobbed. Shaking his head, he pushed the elves away and ran off. Unable to keep up with his swift, though awkward steps, the elves soon gave up the chase. Sylvan slid underneath the roots of a large elm tree and fell asleep. Having eluded the elves on their own turf, he slept contentedly until the sun rose the next day. A squirrel dropped a nut in his direction and ran off. Sylvan searched his surroundings for some berries to go with the walnut, while avoiding being seen by an elf. Following the squirrels, he tracked the location of the walnut tree and began gathering his breakfast. The sound of running water filled his ears and took his collection to a crystal-clear stream rushing through a patchwork of ferns. On the other side of the water, he spotted several wild blueberry bushes. Bugs and others small creatures adorned his pathway as he crossed the current to forage. In this manner, he continued several months until the first snowflakes fell and he stopped to reconsider his arrangements for the upcoming winter. Instead of returning to Robin's camp, he began piling leaves and bedstraw around the roots of the elm. He retrieved a few logs, dragging them across the carpet of moss to block out potential snowdrifts. A small family of rabbits hibernated in his quarters and kept the place warm. He learned new hunting skills from watching the raccoons and occasionally they shared each other's catch, depending on who had the most luck. Sometimes Sylvan nonverbally called a prey into a site to be captured. He followed the rhythms of the wilderness around him, leaving in this uninterrupted melody of comings and goings for over two years.

Occasionally, he ventured into the encampment and chatted with Marie. He could watch her movement like any other creature living in the vicinity. Sometimes she stayed in the castle and other times she slept with Robin. Sensing her whereabouts, he timed his appearances to suit Robin's absences. Whenever Marie became agitated by the local violence, he disappeared into the woods. Over time, she ceased asking questions and attempting to define Sylvan's activities to fit her lifestyle.

When his blue tunic became too small, he traded with Marie for blue cloth and sewing lessons. He gave her a basket of walnuts, which made her feel that she had found a bargain. Overtime, he traded watercress, sorrel, blueberries, and fish for other items. One day he brought a rabbit, which had broken its neck in a fall. Marie paid him handsomely for the animal, which she put in a stew prepared for Robin's anticipated arrival. Jingling his coins in the pocket of his tunic, he returned to his abode and placed his stash next to the leprechaun's pot of gold.

Crierwy knocked politely on the stump of tree placed next to his domain. Noting the dazzling colors looping overhead in the mists, she muttered under her breath, "Oh, another Rainbow Child."

Sylvan emerged from his berm and asked, "Where's the dragon?"

Bending over the lad to reach eye level, she returned his question, "How about trading your wares with the Pooles in Wales?"

"Who are the Pooles?"

"My half-brothers and half-sisters. They live near ponds."

"What do they want?"

"Cloth from Marie."

"She has plenty. I can deal. It will drive Robin nuts."

"True, he could use some encouragement. Henry II depends on his raids." Sniffing the vapor in the air, she continued, "I noticed the rainbow hanging above your door. Did the leprechauns hide with pot here?"

"It matches Elissa's scales," he answered, peering in the woods behind her for signs of the golden Sea Dragon Queen.

"Don't give it away," she advised. "Gold represents the life force of the planet. Over time, you will learn how to connect with that currency without the assistance of the mineral kingdom."

"The leprechaun told me that when he brought in the pot. I wasn't sure that I wanted it. I couldn't eat it. The pot took up valuable space and it doesn't keep the place warm in winter." A shudder ran down his spine, before Sylvan remarked, "Robin's men might kill me for it, if they knew. I've seen how they fight and heard their talk."

"All the more reason to stay out of their way," Crierwy said with a wink.

Gazing into space, Sylvan hugged himself gently as if warding off a cold snap. A rabbit hopped in the underbrush and Sylvan's shivers went away. Composing himself, he focused on the warm breeze rippling through the airy ferns. After Crierwy left, he went to work. Crierwy appeared a few weeks later and he handed her the cloth. Accepting some fish for the exchange, he rushed to Robin's camp with his loot. For a moment, he froze at the sight of the men loitering around the campfire. Dirty, hungry, and weary from their last attack, the overwhelming smell of the fish in Sylvan's hands filled their nostrils. In comparison, Sylvan wore a clean blue tunic. Instead of wearing tights, he lined his pants with strings on the sides for wrapping up his catches. Meeting their stares, Sylvan immediately erupted into a hearty, bear-like hawk, "Fresh fish! Anyone want fresh fish!"

A fat friar approached Sylvan. "Where did you get the fish?"

"Wales."

Turning aside to the men, the friar told them, "The man said that whales gave him the fish."

One of the men by the fire made the sign of the cross over his face. "Blessed be."

Several men by the fire tossed coins at Sylvan's feet.

"We'll take the lot," the friar announced. "I have some monks to feed."

Sylvan handed the fish over and gathered the stilled coins near his feet. After tucking them in his pocket, he politely bowed and waved as he dashed back to the forest. Consumed by their desire for the fish, no one pursued Sylvan. Safe inside a dense thicket, he watched the operations of the camp from afar.

The next day, he disguised himself as a gardener and trimmed the vine on the trellis leading to Marie's room. A route often used by both Marie and Robin for late night adventures. Pruning his way to the top, he fell through a window to the sound of walnuts rustling inside his pack.

"Where have you been?" Marie asked in a demanding tone. Remaining seated in her chair, she looked down at him as he assumed a completely different posture on the castle floor. Sylvan quickly reached inside his pack for his bundle of nuts.

"Feeding the poor," he offered.

"It's only the gardener!" a guard yelled from three stories below.

Marie hurried across the room to gather rolls of cloth for the trade. Waving the guard off, she shouted, "It's okay. I don't think he's broken anything." Then she prudently left the window to retrieve her walnut booty. Lowering her voice, she dryly commented to herself, "He's only gathering his nuts."

Sylvan overheard her whispers and glared at her. He repackaged the cloth to fit inside his knapsack and slid down the trellis without further incident. Feigning injury under the nose of the guards, he faked a limp past the sterile walls of the castle yard. Once outside of the city gate, he raced back to his lush forest.

Glistening in the sun, Elissa stretched in a small meadow on the other side of a dense thicket. Awed by her beauty, he ran to her. Sylvan softly patted her snout as he dropped his knapsack on the ground.

"You'd have an easier time, if you were a troubadour," she remarked.

Stepping back a few steps, he questioned, "Where can I learn to play?"

"Take some of your coins to the lute shop located four miles away. He'll teach you how to dance too."

Sylvan left the dragon for the excitement of the lute shop. After storing the cloth in his shelter, he began his journey. By dusk he reached the store and entered when no one was in site. An elderly man with a twinkle in his eye greeted Sylvan.

Putting his instrument down on the counter, he peered down at the lad. With a slight smile, he told him, "Oh, I've heard about you. So you want to play now."

Without a word, Sylvan eagerly nodded his response.

"Here take this," he said as he accepted a few coins. "You must practice with the abbey choir, otherwise you'll stand apart from the crowd. If you play in the woods, someone might hear you. We'll store your lute in the chapel to be on the safe side. Come here every noon and we'll find someone to dance with you too."

Learning a song with a few chords, Sylvan accepted the storeowner's offer to spend the night. The next day, he placed his lute in the chapel and ran back to work. Meeting his instructor at noon, he practiced while the noise from the choir muffled his awkward plucks. Gradually, his tunes began to sound like music and he joined the choir.

One day, an arrow whizzed over his head and nearly hit the instructor. Sylvan recognized the marks on the arrow, and climbed out of the window with his lute. Silently noting his response, the others in the room followed him. "The arrow is from Robin. He usually fires a warning shot when he is three miles away."

"His warning almost hit us both," his instructor observed as he ruefully rubbed his head.

"He aims to kill. His messenger must be having an off day," Sylvan replied. "The first hit is meant to hold everyone in place, until the others arrive. Terror gives them the advantage."

"What do you suggest?"

"Present ourselves as wandering troubadours and sing outside the castle walls. We must make ourselves look merry."

Donning several colorful scarves from a vendor near the castle, the abbey choir altered their attire. They threw off their robes and covered themselves with the scarves. Having such a great time singing and dancing, they almost forgot their troubles. The sound of the raucous could not be ignored and Henry II invited them to dinner.

Marie sent her guard to greet them. "Oh please grace our meal with your merry."

"Do you mean Mother Mary?" one of the scarfed men questioned seriously. The noised altered his ability to hear the message precisely. Unconsciously slipping back into his former role as priest, he continued to further the entertainment in the present.

"Say Grace," another man said, mesmerized by the display of sound and color.

"She didn't come with us," a third man shrieked. "I hope that we didn't leave her playing in the abbey."

"No, wait. I see her," someone said above the din.

Dancing her way through the crowd, Grace stepped forward to intercede for the others. Before she spoke, a guard questioned her, "Would you like to borrow my tights for the night?"

"Whatever I can do to blend in," the sister answered.

Sylvan took his lute and excused himself. Explaining that he had another engagement in the forest, he left before anyone recognized him. He promised, "I'll come get you in the morning, provided that they don't give you permanent residence."

Returning to the grounds as a costumed musician, Sylvan covered himself with a fresh, dead bear and traded with Marie.

"You must bring your merry men around more often. Now that I understand the score, we can cut out Robin the middle man."

"Henry invited us to stay," a merry man said with a light hop. "We'll have more time to create costumes and dance numbers."

Marie added, "Henry wants them to come with him to Aquitaine, where they will create the Basques."

Chapter Six

2013

"THE BOOK *FAREWELL, America* served as a decoy for the 1968 election," Joe told Tobias. "The Crusades targeted ports along the Mediterranean Sea, especially those owned by the Maghreb. Crusaders ran Dallas at the time of the JFK assassination, and the jackal came there. Unlike De Gaulle, he opposed the Maghreb and orthodoxy. As a vet from Korea, the elite force within the Pentagon hired him to run interference."

After the destruction of Gondawanland, the intruders divided into the Oran and Caspian cultures. Much of the Atleantean infiltration came from the Caspians. When Atlantis sank, they fled to northwestern Africa. They joined forces with the Grays and established the Phoenician trade routes, which enslaved world populations. On February 17, 1989, the collective signed a Treaty to Constitute the Union of the Arab Maghreb. The Union included nations such as Mauritania, Tunsia, Algeria, Libya, and Morocco.

The Orans countered the denizen known as Orin. Joe and Tobias had met Orin, the raptorgryph during their excursion to Iron Mountain, Arkansas. A writer for the Orans, Ann Rynd, focused on another place called Iron Mountain in her book *Fountainhead*. Joe had recently finished building an interface for a company that used Rynd's Iron Mountain to shred their documents. They assumed that the headquarters for Rynd's Iron Mountain could be found in Germany, possibly close to the place where Gilgamesh's ancestors attacked the base of the archangels. Located near Angles, Germany, the base harbored the descendants, who later became targets for World War II concentration camps. For every two hundred Jews, the Nazis collected one angel. Another writer, who served the United India company patriots, alluded to the *Odessa File* created on the celestials living on the earth-plane. The jackal had been one of these targets, set up in a military operation to detour the Franks from handing France Foreign Legions and Jews to the Orans in Algeria. After realizing the futility of the operation, the jackal turned on those who had set him up. The United India company never forgave him for breaking his programming, which had been seeded in the genetic code since the attacks on Angles, Germany.

"This brings us to the group, who targeted your plane, Tobias," Joe explained. "The slave traders from Gondwanaland do not want people to recover their spirit."

"Then the spirit of 1776 is in danger too," Tobias surmised. Another thought crossed his mind, as he cradled the phone over one shoulder and stretched his legs over the desk. "So if JFK and myself represent little fish in a big, oil-soaked pond, who goes after the fish that feed off of us?"

"Shortly after the president's assassination, cannibals in Africa devoured a paddling progeny of a wealthy oil-baron."

"Looking for Dr. Livingston, I presume?" Tobias questioned. Livingston represented the interests of the United India company patriots. Company men often joked about meeting in remote Africa for handshakes. Children's cartoons portrayed the scene as the Stanley-Livingston trip, where the two men find each other in passing. Recalling the humorous line, Tobias commented, "He must have been going upstream. Would you attend a business meeting with cannibals after a national tragedy?"

"Nope, obviously he fed a bigger fish."

"Nobody heard that tree fall in the forest."

"It's not our forest."

"True. Yale is written all over most of the Pacific Northwest wood."

"Yes, it is enough to make a volcano vomit all over eastern Washington."

"Go for it, Tobias."

"Don't give me any ideas, Joe. I have finally figured out why all the undergraduate psychology texts obsess about the remarkable African customs."

"I think that Bush's ancestor Pepin fell into the wrong crowd there. The bigger fish served him for dinner as a Roman Empire dish. When it came down to the Bushes, the Africans named a snake after the clan. They called it *Lachesis,* or master of the bush."

"That's why Truman said, *if you can't stand the heat, get out of the kitchen.*"

"Truman was in quite a stew."

"Hades provided the heat."

The two men said goodbye and ended the call. Tobias gazed at the photo on his desk showing Orin wrapping his great wings around the three of them. Michelle, his wife, had led the trip. Wishing to renew connections with the Linkhorns, she traced their whereabouts from President Lincoln's descendants. Before marrying the sister of Simon Bolivar, the president had the name Linkhorn. When the Orans murdered his family, Abe changed his name to enter politics.

Now a popular amusement park had claimed a similar mountain for their own and promoted mass vaccination. Named for the ascended beings known collectively as Metatron, the Materhorn had been replicated in Southern California. The translation of Meta- and Mater- matched the concept of *matter*. The ancient Greeks deliberated over the topic of matter. Like Gilgamesh's Epic, they failed to fathom how being from nonbeing came from being, and vice-versa. Though Noah had attempted to tell Gilgamesh that it didn't matter, Gilgamesh pursued the question to the end of the earth, almost bringing the end about, literally.

As Gilgamesh obsessed over nonbeing, his predecessors attended medical schools in Africa. Unlike the wise women burned at the stake during the middle ages, the witch-doctors enjoyed unrivaled reverence. A botanical expert in his field equated slander to modern-day witchcraft. Sowing the seeds of gossip and innuendo all over the western hemisphere, the witch-doctors kept their reins on the slave trade and captured the spirits of world governments. Victimized by the continual onslaught of disinformation and coverups, the United States became trumped by a genetically modified candidate from New York. Posing as a politician-professor, he brought the poison-thought forms to grotesque proportions.

Tobias left his home office and searched for his wife in the kitchen. Having assisted a new mother deliver a healthy eight pound boy at three in the morning, she required a hearty breakfast before unwinding from her day. Tobias hugged and kissed Michelle before assisting with food preparation.

Meanwhile, he broached the topic of his previous conversation. "I just finished talking to Joe. We all need protection from the African witch-doctors."

"Do you mean General Aziz of Mauritania or is it that guy that runs Libya?" Michelle questioned casually as she reached inside the refrigerator for some homemade apple butter. "Well, you know how competitive medical schools can be. Just remember how many first years raced to get the biggest cadaver."

"They learned how to cut the fat," Tobias responded. "The rest of us failed to develop an allergy to formaldehyde. I just have a sensitivity to plastic zip-locks; the aroma follows you everywhere."

"Are you sure that it is not the cup of Borgia?" she questioned. "Those vampires have their own agenda."

"Don't they run NATO or something? We need protection from NATO, too."

"Let's change the topic before I lose my appetite."

Munching on pancakes smothered with apple butter, Michelle thoughtfully revived the subject. "I have a plan. We go underneath the radar of these failed institutions."

"How?"

"By counting our blessings. Would you like to live in Africa and stand behind a boiling pot all day?"

"It's hot there already."

"Sweltering with mosquitoes."

"True, the poison that they brew might one day end up in the stinger of a mosquito. Can you imagine dominating world trade, and being retired by a poisoned mosquito?"

"You and I know how to deal with rancid bug bites, but these people just make bigger bugs with bigger stingers. The Olympians are out of habitant in the jungle."

Tobias leaned back in his chair with a low whistle. "There goes the Gaud DNA."

"The jungle served only as a limited time offer for the *Boys From Brazil*, which is an altercation from the boy next door or *Boys of Summer*."

"Do you mean the song by the Eagles?"

"Who else pushed the American Revolution?"

"Are you sure that it wasn't the sexual revolution, Michelle?"

"We gotta get back to the garden somehow, and it isn't just Eden. The human form demands something more earthly than Mount Olympus. Something more divine, and less troublesome."

"Like Arkansas."

"Well, I've *Never Been to Spain.*"

"After Queen Isabella persecuted Michael the Archangel, who would feel safe there?"

A representative of the Vlad the Impaler-Roman Empire conglomerate, Queen Isabella, served to bring Hades to earth. Lending three ships to Columbus and his enterprise, she succeeded in changing the name of two continents from Connecticut to America. Michael brought the recipe from Chalice Well to Puerto Rico. The governor, Ponce de Leon, renamed the concoction the Fountain of Youth and British bankers gave the recipe to the voodoo doctors of South America. When Michael arrived to help the Seven Cities of Cibola, Hades killed him. He stashed the airships of Michael's squadron in a cave, which wasn't located until the investigation following the Holmes Point shooting unraveled the innuendo about a caped crusader. None of the investigators considered the threat a joke, so they searched the area behind the former Baby Doe mine for clues. The jackal traced the connection from the Dallas settlement and located the angel's platforms close to the perpetrator's Neuro lab.

"I know those Ouchita Mountains from Oklahoma, though I wasn't born there like the singer of Three Dog Night. The range extends into Arkansas."

Chapter Seven

"I DREAM IN puns," Tobias admitted to Michelle.

"Joe and Gabriella will be here soon. Rest up while you can," she said, packing her midwifery gear away.

Gabriella, Joe's significant other, had been shouldering most of the company's enterprise since Joe's trip to Arkansas with Michelle and Tobias. One of their projects consisted of building an interface for banking, where US dollars would stay in the terrain. Anticipating foreign interference, the company put the system's hardware in a white vans for greater mobility in an emergency. When terrorism destroyed the bank tower and many buildings in Silicon Valley, Joe and Gabriella hid the interface concealed inside the van. At Iron Mountain, Joe networked with an ancient civilization, which had been providing global security long before money issues divided Gondwanaland.

As the spokesperson for the company prior the onslaught, Joe remained in hiding. The dust had not settled regarding the attack, and none of their enemies had been flushed out. Instead, United Elektra wrote off the mishap as a deduction, whereas Joe's company knew that if they had not mobilized, then they would have been destroyed along with the others. Their interface kept US dollars from being electronically sent overseas. Whoever planned the attack failed to rob the United States of its currency, because of the company's efforts.

Fearing retaliation, they tried to end the negative cycle, but the company could not get its wish. Now Joe and Gabriella sought the security of Tobias's and Michelle's home. Located in the Cascade foothills, Tobias and Michelle had successfully raised their two sons near the sanctity of the Oregon forests.

When Joe and Gabriella arrived, they convened in the living room to elicit more details from the fleeing couple.

"My sources tell me that the Arabs had something to do with the bank in India," Joe explained as he sipped his green tea.

"They settled the area around the Caspian Sea during the time of the pyramid civilizations, Gabriella added. Changing the subject, she observed, "We still may have another attack. This time, we may all be killed."

"Call me, Ishmael," Tobias blurted. "According to history, Ishmael, as the disinherited son of Abraham, started the Arab civilization. However, in *Moby Dick*, Ishmael survives the whale's attack, whereas the Brahmins do not."

Michelle shifted her position on the sofa, and interjected, "In the lore, Ishmael's hand went against everyone and everyone went against him. It became his destiny to fight and be fought. The pre-Civil War satire, *Moby Dick*, depicts Ishmael as a passenger during a ride through some of the roughest waters imaginable."

"Nature loved him," Tobias stated. "I think that Moby Dick the whale moved on."

Gabriella rose from her chair for a glass of water. Exiting the room for the kitchen, she commented, "So all we have to do is ride the tide."

"And put the interface in a coffin and send it out to sea," Joe mused with a wry grin. "Like the documents put in JFK's coffin and dropped in the ocean---Bobby protested the move, but I think that it proved to be the safest place to store them, now that they have recently been recovered."

Gabriella entered the room with her refreshed glass of water. Having overheard Joe's remark, she appeared wide-eyed. "So we put the interface in a tugboat."

"It is easier to do repairs in a tugboat than a coffin," Joe responded.

"Banking tugboats, courtesy of Ishmael," Tobias commented.

"Gotta let the boat drift," Joe observed.

"You mean the signal," Gabriella said, lightly nudging him. "Signal drift is a common occurrence on older radios, which can be used to temporarily hide data. We can do it, Joey. I need to relax."

With a stretch and a yawn, Gabriella announced, "I'm going to bed. You can email the person with the van and tell him about our latest maneuver. Tomorrow, I'll work out the details."

The next morning, Joe rose and found Gabriella typing away at the workstation arranged in the kitchen. Michelle and Tobias prepared breakfast at a nearby counter in the room. Looking over Gabriella's shoulder at her work on the screen, he surmised, "Apparently the Arabs crewed the ships for United India."

"Druids were not whale hunters," Tobias observed. "The whaling industry changed the face of Connecticut, a former druid settlement."

"Without a crew, a ship doesn't sail. In effect, the Arabs own our banking via United Electra. If they pulled their support from the Eye-in-the-Sky bank, then it would fail."

"The currents of money become more apparent when the people account for the labor involved."

"Do you think Gabriel set them up?"

"No, it was Gaud, who displaced Ishmael. Abraham never had the money to pay Ishmael's mother for her labor."

"It's probably how unfair trade practices developed. Even Hitler awarded the mothers of his Nazis with little blue crosses."

"So they turn against nature and God, and take out their frustrations on the dragons of the sea and the rest of His/Her creations."

"I'm surprised Ishmael never developed a complex with such prevalent psychological abuse."

"Some call it the military-industrial-complex."

"It's probably why they had to store the documents of JFK's casket in the sea."

"This why people sang *What the World Needs Now Is Love, Sweet Love* when Arabia appeared at the shooting of his younger brother. Now we could use more mountains and meadows, apparently there was a surplus in 1968."

"It doesn't take long, like the whales."

"Like the Civil War, the United States got caught in another foreign war, one between the Arabs and Divine Nature."

Joe walked over to the picture window and gazed at the Cascade Mountains in the distance. They rose like cathedrals touching the heavens with amassed magnificence. His mecca stood everywhere on this looming horizon. Iron Mountain, Arkansas served as his interface between heaven and earth, providing answers for his soul's search.

"There are many trails," Tobias offered, rolling out the dough for the biscuits. "I always find something nice on every one, something worth the hike."

Joe never responded. Instead, he sighed as he continued to stare in the distance. Gabriella went to his side. Without touching him, she shared his vision. Then she quietly left to join the others for breakfast. Moments later, Joe sat down at the dining table in the next room. Silently, he helped himself to some scrambled eggs and biscuits. After helping the others clean up, he climbed the stairs to the guest room for a midmorning nap.

In his dreams, he climbed aboard a flying ship, like the one Peter Pan captured from the pirates of Never Never Land. The half-eaten carcass of Captain Hook floated in the sea below. An alligator from a Florida amusement park burped audibly, and the noise reached the ears of the passengers on the airship. Bound for Wales, the words uttered by Tobias echoed through the cloud-studded sky. "Call me, Ishmael."

"No, that's not my name," Joe protested. "I want to change. I promise not to feed the gators."

"They must forage. Keep rising above this situation, Joe. There's no place left to go but up."

As the ship flew through the sky, Joe watched the seas below. Swimming mermaids replaced the alligator scene. They dotted the waves like punctuation points.

"Remember, Joe, it's all about recovering the fish. Hook is done poisoning the waters."

A nonthreatening whale came and made a big splash. The spray touch the curved, wooden planks of the boat's undersides. The hint of salt lingered on Joe's lips, as the water droplets fell back into the sea. Peter Pan twirled on a beam overhead. His lost boys slid down the rope ladders and skated over a slippery deck. He stopped dancing on the riser and hollered to his passengers, "Tell Wendy to tell us a story, now that we have the gold."

A multidimensional woman emerged from the crowd. Joe recognized her from previous dealings with apparitions. After a quick wink at Joe, she peered at Peter from the deck. "Call me, Wendy."

Joe nodded his agreement. "Beats Ishmael and we know where he went."

The multidimensional woman shook her head sadly. "It wasn't Wales."

The whale ejected water through its spout and a rainbow appeared in the mists.

The multidimensional woman spoke for the whale. "He says that he can make a rainbow anytime he wishes."

"It's not an illusion," Joe insisted.

Fairies appeared from the shades of color in the sky. They fluttered over to the ship and danced a few feet above.

"We must be getting close to Wales," Peter observed. He shaded his eyes as he glanced at the next horizon.

Joe looked down at the wooden planks and saw his shadow emanating from his feet. Laughing at the black form, he puffed out his chest with pride. He looked at the multidimensional woman and noted her missing shadow. "I am real and you are not."

"Rainbows don't have shadows," she told him, crossing her arms over her chest. "Never take me for granted."

Joe appeared crestfallen by his failure to understand.

The multidimensional woman uncrossed her arms and softened her demeanor. "Not everything you see is real and not everything real is seen."

"OK, I'll think about that one," Joe promised.

Tobias's words filled the atmosphere, "Joe, get your thyroid function checked. The ability to separate illusion from the authentic lies in the thyroid, which is about self-expression."

Michelle added her voice, "Thyroid development occurs between two and seven years old. Maybe you missed something."

Joe responded, "I built rockets out of tinker toys at the time."

"Joe, it's all an illusion. Where are you going?"

Joe faced the multidimensional woman and told her, "Wales."

"Great, Joe. Leave your delusions and nevers of your life with Hook. Never say never, Joe."

Peter and the flying airship faded into the mists of Joe's consciousness. Only the sparkling form of the multidimensional woman remained as he awoke. Before she drifted out of the room, she told him, "Joe, it's time to play."

"*...And the men and women the players in it,*" he thought as he opened his eyes, half-quoting a line from Shakespeare. Beginning as *All the World's a stage...*, the dialogue coursed through his mind like a river. Getting our of bed, he gazed at the snowcapped features on the rocky knobs in the distance. Although magical in shape and form, they were very real. A weight fell from his shoulders as he took Gabriella's place at the workstation.

Chapter Eight

AFTER JOE AND Gabriella completed the project, they returned to their homes in California. Together, they lacked the strength to address the issue in its entirety and fathom the enormity of the problem. Tobias continued to shine in his work as a Naturopathic physician and made a good living. Years ago, a childhood friend encouraged him to leave the Dallas-Fort Worth area when violence erupted in the region. Tobias decided to stay in the Pacific Northwest and avoid the chaotic dynamic. Instead, he used his medicine to restore order in pathologic biological systems.

As he looked over the lab results sent by his colleagues, he noted the decline in titers and Hepatitis C titers with the help of nutritional therapeutics. Another Naturopathic physician had successfully turned around a hemophiliac case with measurable results. The texts claimed that blood clotting factors could not be stabilized, because genetics made the pathology permanent. This proved not to be the case. Another Naturopathic physician beat terminal brain cancer and third-generational prostate cancer, which had been fatal in the first two generations.

Surveying the clinic's documentation over the years, Tobias became alarmed at the trend following the invasion of Russian-Chinese planes in US airspace. Though the nations never claimed to be working together publicly, Russian war planes almost landed in San Francisco last year. The incident occurred when all the servers went out in the area. Meanwhile, China continued to threaten US bases protecting Japan. Korea, which Tobias still considered unified despite the war, sided with China's ambitions. Local businesses filled the ranks of the software and electronics industry with green card nationalists, while discouraging the local talent.

More chaos, he thought as he read the latest email from Joe. He noted that Joe's operation could go upside down. An incident with the Russian-Chinese-Korea pact could lock the region's money in the Eye-in-the-Sky building of United India, where the Kochi state government religiously worships snakes.

Meeting Michelle for lunch at a cafe down the street, he posed the question, "Michelle, do you think that it would be easy to get a religious snake-worshipper to help you get your money back?"

"Isn't that an oxymoron, Tobias?" she asked. "From a medical point of view, the reptilian brain would be shut down in fear-based greed. If all they have is a reptilian brain, then all negotiations would be futile. Remember, you can't reason with a two-year-old. You wait until three to teach social skills."

"Good, I'm glad that I have your assistance in seeing reality here. I don't have the strength to see much more," Tobias remarked, waving a hand in the air with a sense of resignation.

"That's why we've kept our family under the radar. We never encouraged the boys to shine. We taught them to make life-supporting decisions."

"If they die getting shot down in class, then they've flunked," Tobias said pointedly. "Their schools survived several lock-downs by the time they left for college in remote areas."

Pushing away her food, Michelle opted for a doggie-bag. As scrapped the portion from the dish and into the box, she mentioned, "I'm leaving the clinic for a more mobile operation, like Joe's company."

Tobias nodded silently and rose from the table to pay the bill. Leaving separately, Tobias and Michelle headed back to work. A colleague greeted him at the door. Handing an opened envelope to Tobias, he announced, "We've been audited for all our chart notes for the past four years. The insurance companies claim that it is part of keeping up with the socialized medicine laws."

Tobias accepted the note and checked his schedule for the rest of the week. A fourth of his patients had cancelled due to immediate transfers or job loss. Walking into his office, he sat down and turned on his laptop. He skimmed the latest bulletin from a group of professionals. One of their colleagues had recently passed away. Like the other three preceding this event, the deaths were wrapped in sudden, mysterious circumstances.

The next month, Michelle handed Tobias an opened envelope. Stepping inside the living room to avoid getting wet in the storm, he quickly seized the letter. State auditors wanted information on her business, which had significantly declined over the past two quarters.

"Do you ever feel like you are only a mouse in someone's controlled experiment, where mad scientists alter a few variables and measure the effects afterwards."

Tobias put the letter down, and sat down in a soft chair. "Michelle, it used to be that when you turned a case around, the conventional allopaths said congratulations. Now they radiate the homes, contaminate the water, add more drugs, and nuke the patient before they ever reach the lab, another place which further hassles them by losing data or creating issues with insurance. I know, because I went to school with them. With the mismanaged road construction in the region, most patients arrived four times more stressed than usual. I just got a letter from another insurance company telling me that they won't pay unless I get the office visits down another twenty minutes, which is already twenty minutes less than how we were trained in school."

"I agree," Michelle rejoined, sitting down across from Tobias. "A client just received a letter saying that an insurance hacker had made off with the notes on eleven million customers."

Tobias stood and retrieved his notes on an amethyst bracelet, that he once owned. Having given the object to a relative of the World War II pilot for a museum, he decided, "No that we've escaped military medicine, we must go back to the pyramid civilizations for clues."

"Start with the jackal," Michelle told him as she headed to the kitchen to prepare dinner.

"Why the jackal?" Tobias asked, following her.

"It was a Nazis code used to describe an individual, one that they wanted to set up like Oswald with Jack Ruby. Ruby became the mouse for their cancer research, which they also wanted to hide."

"Both of their associates researched cancer. Then Oswald marries the daughter of a Russian general, a pope dies unexpectedly, a US president gets shot, the Russian premier finds exile, and a Russian dissident emerges in the US with *Cancer Ward*. By the looks of his beard, the writer appears orthodox and he provided no solutions, only fear. I've read the book, he didn't even try botanicals, nutrition, or quantum medicines."

"See the pyramidal structure," Michelle advised as she began chopping vegetables. "Traumatized cells go carcinogenic. It is a growth, which we don't need." Turning away from Tobias as she ran cold running water over the produce, she remarked, "The ability to distinguish illusive growth from authentic growth assumes even greater significance."

"The pyramid scheme was established by the Phoenicians. They came from Iceland to rule the Mediterranean region."

"Were they the ones who scattered hearts along the routes?"

"Like the ones the aliens carved out at the pyramids?"

"There's your trauma. It pertains to the Shroud of Turin."

"The Holy Roman Empire drafted a Templar knight for human sacrifice."

"Was the image made by radiation or perfuse human trauma?"

"Radiation is as old as Atlantis. The Serpentines radiated the Arctos civilization and almost destroyed this group of Atlantean survivors. They intended to kill those who knew the truth."

"The Mediterranean, Black, and Caspian Seas formed the Tethys Sea in ancient times. The Caspian Sea became landlocked and a canal connects it to the others."

Known as Grays, entities between the light and dark beings, the Phoenicians capitalized on the trauma created near the ancient Tethys Sea. While the Serpentines seized the souls of their hypnotized prey, the Phoenicians stole their belongings for trade along the Mediterranean Sea. The overzealous medical profession along the African coast bargained for the body parts, which filled their boiling pots with more dark magic. Those Grays on the east side of the Caspian Sea learned the art of illusion from the Serpentines. The Grays on the western end became the Maghreb and adopted Ishmael. These Arabs fled into northwestern Africa after a spaceship wiped out the tower of Babel. The Gauds on Mount Olympus didn't care for the competition and sent a destroyer. The severe trauma resulted in severe language barriers, depending on location during the time of the attack. Many survivors regressed to baby talk.

Overtime, the illusionists became dark and rivaled the incarnations of the Atlantean dark wizards. After destroying the Midearth through a portal in Narni, Italy, Sauron established an outpost in France with the Salish descendants of Nimrod. Nimrod's ancestors had attacked several the angel's platforms. Only one of the landings enjoyed success. These victors became known as the archangels because they had managed to bridge the heavens with the planet. In those days, the ancients referred to bridges as arches.

Staying light on their feet, the angelic angles from Angles, Germany cultivated a civilization of Anglos to protect western Europe from the anti-MidEarth operations stemming from Sauron's outpost in France. Sauron intended to erase any trace of Atlantean memory from the local Celtics and Gauls, generally through genocide and domestication with the Roman Empire.

Finishing her task at the kitchen sink, Michelle questioned, "So what about the pyramids?"

"They employed slave labor to bury the leaders of the civilization. The illusion hid the perpetrators from view. Aliens won the intergalactic wars and buried the evidence under the monuments. Only the base at Iron Mountain survived."

"So what are we going to do about our economic loss and looming destruction?"

"Let go of the loss of Russia-China-Korea," he replied. "They are on a sinking ship, whereas we conservatively move forward."

"It's about the technology, isn't it?"

"They have recreated the problems of Atlantis and want to import the ego-driven technology," he remarked. "You and our adult-children must stay under the radar. Avoid the competition."

"There's still a chance that our fortune may run dry."

"All the more reason to avoid being pulled into a fight with them. They have already invaded to an irreversible degree. Don't accept their help; it's a Trojan horse."

"Even Kuan Yin wouldn't support them. They refused her gifts. The civilization is unbalanced in terms of yin and yang."

"Let's keep our positivity underneath the surface, Tobias," Michelle suggested. "We are in transformation."

"It beats Nostradamus," Tobias commented.

"He provided the headlines for Germaine's work, which at the time, could not be stopped."

"Germaine's minions carried out the self-fulfilling prophesies, sorta like inside information on Wall Street."

"They're operated by the same organization."

"Now you see the mess we are in."

Chapter Nine

AS MICHELLE MOBILIZED her practice, former clients created a win-win situation where they could obtain care without feeding the Russian-China-Korea alliance. They appreciated being more than a datapoint in foreign affairs, especially programs bent on spiritual and planetary oblivion. Remaining conservative, their combined families focused on achieving a greater level of health for their future.

Donna and her husband, Eli, came to visit while Michelle attended a delivery. Tobias had met Donna through Joe. Joe encountered Donna from her sidekick, Carrie, an astrophysicist working at an university in Maryland. Both Tobias and Joe often consulted with Donna, a geophysicist from Woodsport with a knowledge of planetary electromagnetics and fields. Past events had compelled Donna and Eli to risk exposure as Eli's law firm researched atomic warfare manufactured by Americans subject to hypnosis. Their investigated had led them past the Environmental Protection Agency and to the shadowy realms regarding French Intelligence and the American Revolution.

"It goes back to Stirling Castle in Scotland," Donna explained as they helped Joe pile his chopped wood. The moist dew hung in the air as a thick, gray cloud blanketed the verdant foothills. She raised her head to sniff the moisture content for intruders, then she resumed. "The castle was originally a fort hill called Ludeu. It served the same network as Iona."

Deviating from the subject, Eli stepped forward and explained, "Working with the New York Attorney General's office, we learned that the original Mayflower passengers became Paine's political prisoners. Considered as another slave ship, the Mayflower ranks with the Arab's fleet from northwestern Africa."

"The jackal, in United India's movie, portrays a US vet from Korea, who gets setup as an assassin in France. As a teen, he worked for Admiral Byrd's outfit in Alabama. He beat the programming and won support from the Blue Angels, JFK's covert Air Force unit."

Tobias threw a log on the pile. Landing on the stack with a loud clank, the sound rebounded off the mists in a manner that seemed to make the listeners feel protected. Joe smiled as he secured the logs in their positions.

"Eventually neocons took over the squadron and gave it to Nazis," Eli added.

Joe eyed him carefully. "What does this have to do with my project."

"The jackal submitted the deeds for this family property in New York. It relates to the vice-president son's investigation of the real estate in the Annapolis area, where the jackal's family lived. They helped create the Pentagon after the American Revolution."

Donna paused and wiped the beaded perspiration from her forehead. Shaking her wet leather glove, she added, "The United India company murdered those serving our nation's first capitol and swept it to Philadelphia, near Dallas's occult lodge where Benjamin Franklin had been a member."

"Torture chambers for your ancestors lie buried on the New York property," Eli stated.

Tobias glanced at the Cascades on the distant horizon and removed his thick mitts, "Now we can see what happened to Connecticut. Michelle and I can break it to Joe, gently."

"It is far worse than what happened with slaves from the African trade. The Department of Justice can't handle it."

"How about a cup of organic hot chocolate," Tobias proposed in light of the situation.

Leaving the scenery for the warmth of a special brew, the threesome waited in the kitchen for the almond milk to steep. Joe inoculated their mugs with a touch of cardamom, ginger, and cinnamon. Pouring the hot almond milk over the organic, unsweetened cocoa powder, he stirred the contents of the three cups.

"The coat of arms for the Ludeu bears a white unicorn. It matches the Sun card, number 19, in the tarot deck."

Tobias laughed, despite the intensity of their discussion. Sipping his concoction, he questioned, "A white unicorn at a Scottish castle?" Then he dryly remarked, "I'll have to talk to my Sasquatch about this."

"Don't bother, we've figured that the unicorns are related to the Caspian white horses," Donna added, tasting Tobias's spontaneous formulation. Then she explained, "After Gondwanaland collapsed, the spirit of the women from that civilization inhabited white horses, known as Caspians. A pyramid located near the Caspian sea attracted the horses, who ran wildly over the steppes. The forebears of King Arthur mated the horse with unicorns from Scotland, intending to strengthen the spirit after witnessing the demise of Tepe Giyan. Sicilian mobs invaded the terrain to behead the horses. Not only did the mob intend to destroy the divine feminine, but they wanted to obliterate any trace to the Gondwanaland civilization. Gondwanaland kept watch on the Eye-in-the-Sky as a port for airships like the Black Knights."

"Scientists have dated the satellite dubbed the Black Knight to 13,000 years old."

"To shorten a long story, the surviving Druids from Ludeu went to present-day Alabama."

"Apparently, Lynard Skynard knew what he was talking about."

The originator of the song *Freebird* came from Alabama and died under mysterious circumstances in a plane crash at the height of his career. His songs stirred the enemies of his intergalactic ancestors. Ascended artists from Andromeda settled Ludeu in Scotland. Under the flag of Zeus's black eagle, the Roman legions decimated the fort and replaced it with Gowan Hill. The House of Brus took over the region with the help of William the Conqueror. Serving as a Trojan horse, they restored the unicorn to its habitant. Their efforts became noticed by Sicilian mobs, who razed the castle. The relations in present-day Alabama recreated Stirling Castle and brought the spirit of the unicorn to the landmass known as Connecticut.

When Roman legions, under the guise of the British Empire, invaded the continent for the War of 1812. They crucified the land owners in the streets of New York and altered the records. The White House almost let them in, but Madison changed his agenda at the last moment and burned the place. The Holy Roman Empire wanted to keep its holdings in the district.

A descendant of Michael, the archangel, King Oswy, worked with the Scottish Kings, Gerwyn and Fergie, to supply warriors to fight legions in Rome. Having been part of the early Christian-catacomb network, Ludeu oversaw rescue operations. Michael's archangels airlifted many people before they reached the jaws of the lions in the coliseums. Eventually Constantine gave up sacrificing his relations and their supporters.

Evacuees came to the Connecticut landmass, where they remained unidentified for many generations. Meanwhile, the Roman soldiers established a Black Eagle Trust. The derivative in England became the National Trust. They used confiscated goods to pay assassins and soldiers of the Roman Pentarch. Originally a Tetarch of four empires, Diocletic created the fifth one by placing King Antiochus at Gobleck Tepe. The tepes had once supported the platforms of the archangels. With assistance from King Arthur's great-grandmother, also the great-great grandmother of King Gerwyn, Lady Casper secured the Tepe Giyan until the Russian Revolution displaced the Romanov's Dragon flyers.

"The jackal knew that several members from the House of Brus lost their hearts in New York. He gave us information on the real estate agent working for the Transylvania Land company. To escape the legal system, he's running for president of the United States. The House of Brus had worked with King Oswy and refugees from the catacombs. The Transylvania Land company needed more blood and paid the Grays handsomely for their assistance. The Grays were angry at the jackal for ruining their plans in Dallas and in France."

"We need to get Joe to secure his interface from the Black Eagle Trust," Tobias surmised, after listening to their story. "They rob the planet of its gold by altering the life currency."

"It's lack of trust, metaphorically," Donna commented

"All the more reason for greater security," Eli observed.

"Restore heart to the catacomb network," Tobias commented. "The Tetrarch turned world trade into a heartless operation, literally. The Pentarch served to make fun of it. One leader, Diocletic, served the cult of Dionysus."

"A British occultist reversed the wheel of fortune during World War II. Her operations influenced both British and United States intelligence. The cult of Dionysus became involved."

"That's why Michelle and I run the risk of losing our luck."

"That's why we are hitting a dead wall with tracing Ben Barka's footsteps concerning French intelligence."

"The key is the jackal, otherwise there is no intelligence."

"He moved the United States military from the realms of occultism, which locked the illusionists from the stronghold in Alabama."

"Now that's the spirit of the Unicorn."

"The group America sang about it in the cartoon *Spirit*."

"Oh, the horses of our lives," Donna said with a sigh. "Mustangs, unicorns, and Caspians, oh my."

"That's it! Tobias responded. We must ride with dragons to avoid reversing the wheel of fortune."

"Go back to the Green Dragon tavern and lighten our spirit," Eli mused.

"Have a beer?" Donna questioned.

"Yes, though there's none in the house. Michelle and I have been too befuddle to drink. We'll have to go on a road trip for beer," Tobias admitted.

"Cheers, Tobias," Eli said as he lifted his hot chocolate brew. "Let's cheer up and save some gas."

"I think that we'll have to do more to alter reality than just change our mood," Donna asserted.

"In other words, be the dragon."

"That drank the beer?"

"No, figure out what made Stirling Castle in Alabama so sweet."

"Apparently, they could keep a unicorn."

"And inspire music."

"Alabama went Mobile, too," Michelle said, strolling into the kitchen. She warmed more almond milk and prepared an individualized hot chocolate concoction. "I overheard the last few lines."

"Somehow they reestablished a connection with the Midearth at Bilbo River."

"Right underneath the nose of Real Audiencia, the Spanish trading company littering the route with stolen hearts."

"Real Audiencia represented the interests of the illusionists, which had nothing to do with being real."

"That's why they call estate *real*, so they could win the bet for human souls."

Chapter Ten

"LIFE IS MORE than just another card game to trump," Michelle observed.

"Which is why we have synchronicity and *Animalspeak*," Tobias remarked. "The application places the odds in favor of the living."

"So what do we have to do to keep our luck going?"

"Don't gamble," Donna rejoined.

Tobias studied the design on the kitchen counter and remarked, "We haven't stepped in an Indian Reservation casino ever. The occultists took the reservations over for their programs."

"That was the program. Now all the new computers, including the televisions have backdoors. If you watch them, they watch you. Joe told us," Eli mentioned.

"Who are they?

"Those running the Silk Road. Joe keeps us underneath the radar from the Arabs, who seized Morocco from the Berbers, a descendant of Cain."

"The descendants of Abel made Ishmael one of their own. Abraham's son by Sara just lined the Arab's trade routes with Brahmins or traders. Meanwhile, Cain and Abel continued to fight like yin and yang, caught in Hegel's dialectic."

"Nobody moves forward, except the Celtics. They learned how to ascend and surpass the spiritual traumas that bonded African slaves to their neighbors who sold them, like Bathsheba and her Ethiopian tribe."

"The Boston Brahmins worked for Cain's organization."

"This is why the United States' television networks engross viewers in ongoing violence. By accessing living rooms, they intend to measure the effect."

"Abel proved naive."

"The clothiers as well as the fashion industry are beholden to the Silk Road."

"Our more gullible clients have left," Tobias confessed. "Instead of health care, they are investing in wineries---either by supply or demand."

Michelle looked at Tobias, "Instead of hiding in our home, how about joining my clinic? Pregnant and overworked families do not have time to watch television. My parent-base refuses to turn the devices into baby-sitters. Besides, the children are doing their own coding these days."

The next day, Donna and Eli returned to their cottage in Rhode-Island. Tobias accepted Michelle's offer and made conservative steps to move forward. Sidestepping previous threats, Tobias and Michelle enjoyed success in the eyes of their peers and clients. They brought their clients safely through troubled waters of a contaminated environment.

When inhabitants of the Indus Valley succumbed to water contamination, the practice of medicine changed as a consequence. Pericles sent emissaries from his exile in Tynes to combat the hysteria, which had reach global proportions. Vedic medicine failed in its system of balances under the duress. It worked well with utopic civilizations, but failing currencies bankrupted their moral fortitude. Monetary issues stemming from the collapse of Gondwanaland rendered the inhabitants as defenseless as Abel, a patriarch. Though Pericles traded Greek culture for freedom from the chaos of Athens, he sent Greek medicine to the survivors of the Indus Valley wishing to change. This system of medicine became known as Unani, which meant Greek. It protected inhabitants from the Arachnids infesting the Tree of Life in present day Korea, who the Greeks called insects, literally. When the Tree of Life became restored in present-day Versailles, the Alemanni assumed care of the tree from the sylvans or wood elves. A system of five humors rather than four, the medicine matched the spirit of the intergalactic pentagon. This Greek system of medicine denoted ascendance from the four compass directions guiding the Earth's humors. The fifth dimension reached into the heavens for inspiration, rather than relying on perverted Gauds for assistance with planetary affairs. The third dimension lent substance and depth; the fourth dimension pertained to evolution through time; the fifth dimension accounted for rotational motion, particularly of the earth in relationship to the universe. At this point in history, questions regarding whether the sun rotated around the earth or vice versa became irrelevant.

Associated with Unani medicine from a practicing physician in Pakistan, Tobias refined his botanical formulations to the spirit of the Himalayans. The mandala for the planet ascended from the four faces of Mount Kailash, which meant crystal in Sanskrit. Mount Kailash rose when the Caspian Sea became landlocked from the Mediterranean Sea. Reaching gothic proportions, Cronos partnered with Lucifer. A byproduct named Atlas, rose to counter the negative influence on the planet through the emergence of gravitational force. The magnetized body weighted the inhabitants and secured them to the planet without the bondage of Prometheus. This allowed intergalactic refugees to settle without the notice of Zeus's eagle. Tobias's work ended a negative cycle from the days of Atlantis, named after Atlas.

Late one evening, Tobias hiked to the base of the Cascades. Wearing a headlamp, he found the path in the moonlight. Rather than pitch a tent, he sat on a boulder and gazed at the stars. The daughter of Hades had begun replacing Unani medicine with opium. The Columbus company bought out stores in the same manner that bankers from England commercialized Aqua de Florida. Captured by Peruvian witch doctors, Michael and his concoction underwent alterations. They trapped Michael's spirit in the matrix established by the bankers for Columbus's expedition. The witch doctors stole the water that Ponce de Leon had dubbed the Fountain of Youth and used it in their voodoo ceremonies. Now his colleagues in the shaman world used the substance for protection and clearing. Over time the evil wrought in the substance degraded and lost potency as those from Angles, Germany gained immunity through ascendance. Through the efforts of enlightened beings on the planet, Michael recovered along with the 9/11 generation. Lost in electronic games, young adults swam in a sea of murky mythology. They could not be counted on to see reality, having lost their souls to the illusionists around the Caspian Sea. An exodus of refugees from the genocide in Armenia settled in California and established Las Vegas, the gambling capital of the West. Like their polygamist relations from Arabia, settlers in the area named the mountains according to planets established by aliens. According to the leaders of the cult, the mountains brought them closer to their desired posthumous destinations. The destroyed the Dixie currency, which had replaced the dollar of the United India company with the stamp of the Eye-in-the-Sky.

Tobias searched for the Pleiades cluster in the sky. Also known as the Seven Sisters, the family constellation claimed Mount Cyllene as their home on earth. Their children roamed the region of Arkadia and protected the planet from Hades's minions, who descended from nearby Mount Olympus. The minions ran operations with Mount Athos. Through a series of illusions, they filled in the ranks of the Titanmachy with their own twelve deities. The illusionists exaggerated the rift between Cain and Abel, until Hades stepped in to claim the victim of the rivalry. Only the giants of the sea, the whales, knew the score and Abel's descendants began slaughtering them to destroy the recordkeepers. After sacrificing one of the craftsmen building Solomon's temple, the hall of records closed. Only the survivors of

Atlantis could access the information. Joining efforts with the Lemurian survivors, the Celtics worked with the Druids to bring the souls from Spica and Arcturus to land mass known as Connecticut. Surviving Pleiadeans brought them through the soul transport system reestablished at the four corners region near Las Vegas. They built the Seven Cities of gold from the minerals mined by the dwarves in present-day Wales. Each of the seven sisters had a city of gold, which sustained the earth's spirit for the transport.

Apaches seeded from the pyramid civilizations in Brazil buffered the area from conquerors, which left Mount Athos to conduct military medicine. They attacked Connecticut from the south as Mount Olympus infused Roman legions to invade the east. The Pentarch sent wizards from Solomon's Temple to fund the American Revolution and destroy any survivors of preexisting civilizations. After confiscating the property of landholders, they sacrificed them to the heroes worshipped on Mount Olympus. This broke the Hegelian dialectic in favor of the male-dominated Pentarch, which perpetuated the destruction of the divine feminine. Having left Adam for Lucifer, Lilith entrapped competing females through the endless struggle between Cain and Abel. The fight between two brothers consumed humanity and rendered females without a voice.

Tobias hiked over to the edge of a rocky ledge. Staring into the abyss that reached into the darkened skies, he thought about how the Serpentine agenda to kill the truth would eventually result in the end of the planet. Since the age of three, his father had taught him how to stand on the edge and compose himself. "Now don't jump," his father had instructed him.

Having been a gymnast in high school, his father perpetually searched for those elegant moments of grace under pressure. Tobias simply followed him to the ends of the earth, while his mother provided feeble admonishments from the sidelines. His father's tests taught him confidence. As the artificial constraints of a society governed by fear-based rules left, the clarity that came with being centered in one's position remained. Factoring in the natural elements of wind and rain, the environment outside of the gymnasium posed another set of challenges. The ability to create balance from the elements required the spirit of the heart. Like finding the eye of the storm within a tornado, this skill evolved through testing rather than reading a book on the subject.

At the ends of the earth, the boundary between heaven and earth often became more distinct. When nature diffused the issue, the path became alarmingly unclear. The only place left to go became the heart, the region within that defined what nurtured the self. In removing the heart from their victims, the priests of a society took away the ability to deal with the elements. Those choosing to heal from the blow created another form with the medicine of Iona, which provided Pericles the ability to elude Jacob and his conquests.

Druid priests from Iona stole offshoots of the Tree of Life from the District of the Poker Tree in Egypt. Greek physicians made Unani medicine from the Tree of Life at Iona, which protected the burial site.

The District of Columbia replaced the District of the Poker Tree. Gamblers arrived in Las Vegas. They destroyed the Tree of Life at Versailles when their network assassinated the president at Dallas.

The Celtics had replicas of Metratron's Cube, which Kabalah scholars termed the Fruit of Life. The Celtic carvings surfaced in Scotland during the 1600s. Before the Age of Pericles, an ancient Greek mathematician named Euclid studied the components of Metratron's Cube. Together with the Celtics, the ancient Greeks collaborated at the Egyptian port of Rhacotis, which Alexander replaced with a city bearing his name. The Greeks established a base called Iona, which meant Greek. They adopted Druid knowledge into their own framework and created Unani medicine. Like the Andromedean artisans, some scientists from ancient Greece evolved and ascended through their work.

Chapter Eleven

TOBIAS WALKED DOWN the mountain in the moonlight. The well-groomed trail appeared below his feet as the quartz in the minerals reflected the ambient light. Arriving home, he entered the kitchen to prepare a cup of lavender tea before retiring for the night. In the morning, he responded to a phone call from an Osteopathic physician in New England. Another cohort of Donna's, he shared information with her like a colleague.

"I am picking up where Donna left off," he explained. "She and Eli told us about the latest results of their investigation, and they hit a wall."

"I've hit a wall, too," Joan responded with a touch of glumness in her voice. "I decided to leave my practice. Holistic doctors are dying in Florida under suspicious circumstances."

"It fits the pattern that we've seen here," Tobias told her. "I want to go back to Donna's findings prior the wedding."

After the conversation, Tobias hung up and examined his notes. He sensed that he had picked up Donna's trail on the mountain. The threats on her life extended to the environmental and health professions. Unani medicine would have restored Joseph of Arimathea's group after the Moors crucified seven of the members. His first destination had been Holland, the headquarters for the international group of Donna's investigation.

The Dutch Indies company brought many African slaves to the region formerly owned by the Green Mountain Boys, descendants of Patrick of Ireland. Later claimed as saint, Patrick settled many of his clan in present-day New York to protect them from slavery. Shortly before the American Revolution, Ethan Allen attempted to retrieve his stolen property in New York through the court system. Ironically, the headquarters for international justice remained in Holland to this day, whereas the slaves coming from Haarlem, Holland encountered economic difficulties in leaving Harlem in New York as free individuals. Despite the amended constitution in the United States, invisible chains shackled those descendants of Harlem. According to the history texts, Haarlem arose before Holland in 866 AD. One of the museums in Hague, the Dutch city housing international law, bore the name of an African country. Called Mauritshuis in Holland, the museum resembled the Mauritania in Africa. General Aziz from Mauritania had attacked Tobias's plane during the night of Libya 9/11. The Moors came from Africa through Spain, the sponsors of the Columbus company. They brought their pills with them. Dutch pharmacist used gapers to advertise their drugs, which came from the boiling pots in Africa. Wearing turbans, the Moors gaped at the public with pills on their tongues. Statues of the gapers hung over the pharmacies at places like the Hague and Haarlem. Under the pervasive circumstances, Unani medicine would have been viewed as a threat. Drugged individuals became easy slaves. In contrast, Plymouth devoted an entire section of the heritage site to medicinal botanicals used by the pilgrims. Tobias recognized his favorite plants and sent for seeds for some of the rarer ones. Though abundant in the forests of the 1600's, many of the species inhabited the endangered species lists now. Individuals promoting the native forests made the endangered list as well.

Dissecting the name of the museum, Tobias related Mauritania to Africa and the Shuis to Medina, an extremely wealthy subdivision near Puget Sound. Home to the families funding the World Trade riots in Seattle and Springfield, Oregon, they sponsored a lobbyist who built casinos after NY 9/11. They also promoted genetically modified substances and opposed labeling of organic products, thereby creating an illusion for consumers.

At the end of the trail, Tobias discovered Casolaro's octopus. One leg represented drug and human trafficking. Another leg represented terrorists, such as the KKK and other dark occultists. Another leg pertained to the Silk Road and clothiers. A fourth leg involved social media and scientific thought. For example, the son of a famous clothing line owned a well-known news show and aerospace company. The clothing line belonged to the interests of the Dutch India company, which dictated fashion New York. A fifth leg of the octopus symbolized the aeronautics industry. A sixth leg ran to fossil fuels. The seventh leg reached into the realms of environmental contamination. The eighth leg incorporated widespread violence, which differed from the organizations simply promoting fear.

Dark wizards produced their own tarot deck before the American Civil War erupted. They later came out with their own brand of sexualized rocketry before the space race of the 1960's. Decades afterwards, sorcerers paid handsome movie stars to sexualize weaponry as they preached the science of occultism and charged Mars rovers. Rivals competed in *getting their guns off* for the same woman. Distinct from the snake-oil salesmen representing the interests of oil barons, citizens paid for their addiction.

Tobias glanced at the tall evergreens, appearing black under the starry sky. He looked for signs of his father, who hid in the shadows. They communicated nonverbally, like radio receivers sensing transmitted information. Shying away from notions of extrasensory perception, Tobias knew that the ability to tune in could be taught. His sons and wife didn't communicate like this, however, he found that he could speak with love in this manner. Long ago, his father had taught him how to listen. The dialogue between them amounted to a few one liners, spaced between much action and extended absences.

At the age of four, Tobias watched his father dash for a mountain trail and followed him. Though he could sense his mother holding her breath, Tobias noticed his younger sister tagging him and hurried away without further hesitation. He tracked his father so closely that he had to avoid the orange-colored dust being kicked in the air by his steps. After a few rough climbs and descents, his father finally instructed him, "Climb on your toes." Then he paused for moment to make sure that his younger sister heard the lesson. Satisfied with their coordination, he sprinted away and left them on their own. Tobias contented himself with a small slope, while his sister became enchanted by an even smaller one.

Somehow, by the age of seven, Tobias had learned how to swim by pool hopping in California. Generous acquaintances lent pool time to his mother, who cultivated relationships with a string of pool own- ers. During one family vacation, Tobias raced his father across non- crowded pool at a hotel. After the second race, his father stopped in the shallow end. He quietly instructed, "Put your arm over mine. Now fol- low my stroke. Your hand goes in the water like an arrow." When they moved the next year, Tobias had a built-in pool in his own backyard and made a swim team.

Having a bigger front yard without rose bushes, Tobias talked his father into playing football with him. His father told him that he had played football in college. He advised him, "Look at their stomach. That's is how you can figure where they are going to move next. Watch the middle of their stomach." Years afterward, Tobias learned how to calculate a person's center of mass in physics and remembered his father's advice concerning movement in space.

"When you sprint, get on your toes," his father told him once when Tobias made the track team. His father had been on the track team for two different colleges in California. After watching some wild west shows on the television, his father would rise from the shag rug with the announcement, "I'm going for a run."

Tobias and his younger sister dove in the car before their father sat behind the wheel. He'd drive to a remote, vacant lot at the high school and park. In the dark, they found their way to the locked gate and climbed the fence. Although, they preferred an unlocked entrance, the minor detail did not discourage their play. They ran independent circles without any illumination from a streetlight. Tobias's father always ran faster. Occasionally lapping them, their father would introduce them to someone he met on the track. With a friendly wave, his father and his companions would trot off. They'd meet at the gate and wait for everyone else to finish. Then their father would make sure that they got over the fence after run.

If they ran in the daylight, then they would play on the assortment of gymnastics equipment before reaching the track. Tobias admired how his father turned around on the parallel bars. With a few words, he learned how to dismount with a sense of elegance and grace before landing on the dry, hard, Texas dirt.

If they decided not to run that night, the wild west shows usually inspired a pillow fight. Tobias always tried to get his father's head, while his younger sister held his feet. However, Tobias's dad liked to dance, being very clever with his feet. He could trap both of them between his legs in vise-grip. Sometimes, if Tobias didn't stay alert, his father would catch him with his feet when Tobias walked across the room. However, if his father didn't stay alert, then Tobias could succeed in clobbering his head with a pillow from the couch. This never happened; both Tobias and his father could feel the other out.

If they went horseback riding, his father always managed to sneak in a gallop at the last moment. Something about his finesse always quieted the guide's ire. Only his mother offered a few feeble protests or admonishments, which soon stifled with the elegant show. After his parents separated, his father took him riding in a Dallas park. Although the signs warned riders about returning with a sweaty horse, his father's horse broke out into a gallop as soon as they reached a lawn three times the size of a football field. Tobias saw the usual, subtle dare in his father's eye when he glanced at him from the distance. He wasted no time in letting the horse run at full speed, which made the breeze seem like nothing in comparison. Afterwards, they walked the stallions to cool them down. The horses returned happy with the jaunt and the owners happily noted their content expressions without saying a word.

One day his father stayed after work to play baseball with some people from the office. He came home early, stating that members of the local national football team had pushed them off the field. They walked away from the bullies and dropped the game. Shaking his head as he studied the ground, his father said that the players were overgrown children, and that was all he said about it. After that occasion, Tobias noticed the general erosion of sportsmanship in the world, as play became more competitive and aggressive.

Now that his father had chosen to stay in the shadows, Tobias watched for signs of contact. Sometimes, he left piles of leaves or rocks. Other times, he made a different design with his wood pile. Tobias spent time figuring out the message. After the House-Senate Committee Hearing on the Assassinations, his father had disappeared. The few times that he did show, he arrived late and under the influence of alcohol. His own man, Tobias kept his boundaries and refused to pressure the relationship. The hiatus ended when his children reached their teenage years, and Tobias sensed that his father had entered his vicinity. After a leaving a few signs in the manner of an Indian, his father validated Tobias's perceptions. Deciding that his father had been a gift, Tobias began making recordings with an intuitive for his father to hear, knowing that he could access this electronic device. In this manner, they began to help each other achieve family security.

Chapter Twelve

Tune Reference: *Mack the Knife*

THE STIRLING CASTLE in Alabama worked with the House of Brus to bring evacuees to freedom. The reptilian-brained Romans feared death. In the comparison, the Celtics and Druids understood reincarnation. They viewed death as another transition like birth. For these reasons, the Romans failed to find those hiding in the catacombs.

Studying the literature in his home office, Tobias reasoned that a certain pathologic state would be associated with those forced to live in the twilight zone, the realm of burial chambers. He found that the homeopathic *Belladonna* fit the scenario. The remedy balanced the autonomic nervous system between flight and fight. A common childhood remedy for fevers, *Belladonna* supported rapid and violent growth. Unfortunately, a portion of the population had become so toxic, that they required biotherapeutic drainage to be able to take substances that others found healing.

Other than homeopathics, Michael's platform airships provided the only means to get past the Moors, searching the Mediterranean for people to fill the Phoenician's ships. The Moors supplied the drugs for the Roman parties, which easily deteriorated into orgies. The orgies could be used for extortion and blackmail. Politics in Rome ran according to the latest orgy.

The House of Brus worked with Henry II, as he fed evacuees to Ludeu from Edessa County. Tobias's father gave him information on the file kept by British intelligence. Changing the E to O, a writer for the United India company mentioned the uniformed German officers captured along with Jews. Descended from the platform people, these Germans eluded those countering the Eagles of the American Revolution. These enemies came from Hanover. During WWII, the angels died with the Jews drugged for genocide. Coming from Alabama, his father knew about this. Poverty provided the army with enlistees, intending to beat the dire circumstances of the eventual draft. While Henry II enlisted under William the Conqueror, the Drake family suffered in the draft. The Viking Grays killed off the family and gave the name to an orphan, who championed the United India company for Elizabeth I, daughter of Henry VIII. The war became a matter of survival, rather one between angles and demons. The Vikings found themselves at war with the Spanish demons, after Isabella destroyed Michael's operation. Stranded angels intermarried with the Basque slaves placed in South America and placed Michael's fiery red sword in another dimension. Like other sacred objects on the planet, an individual came to embody the attributes of the artifact.

After Britain betrayed the allied cause in WWI, the angels remaining in Germany wrote about Michael's sword. *The Threepenny Opera* enjoyed so much popularity that the composer could defect from Nazi Germany before the next roundup began. Aware that the United States had become socialist after the attack on Annapolis, the composer found that Jefferson's socialism provided cover from the extremes of communism and fascism. The United India company turned capitalism into an illusion with help from Germaine's chateau operations.

As the songs from *Threepenny Opera* hit Las Vegas, bankers for Vlad the Impaler gridded with the Kennedy compound in Hyanis Port. The patriarch crossed paths with the same Paines interning the early pilgrims fleeing Lord Germaine. Villains from Atlantis bought farmland in Pullayup, Washington and resumed their genetic modifications. Trapped between spiritual predators and witch doctors, the genetics associated with the Conn family druids won. Morgan Le Fay's curse on Bridget resulted in the demise of Kennedy/Linkhorn (Lincoln) offspring. This bought the world more time in retrieving Michael's sword from the Nazca lines.

The House of Brus entered the Tudor line at the time of Henry IV. The mother of Henry IV had a son outside of the relationship with the 1st Duke of Lancaster. When the War of the Roses brought the Henrys to power, the sons of the bards reclaimed Wales. The paternal great-grandfather of Henry VII had been a Brus. Mary, the Queen of the Scots, sent both the Bruces and Henrys to the

Jamestown colony to fight the Transylvania Land company. Her half-sister, Elizabeth, intervened and the pirate Drake also attacked the region. Caught in a three-way tie, the Bruces and Henrys sought help from the Black knights of Italy, who protected the Camelon trade routes taken over by Iona. After the Holy Roman Empire infiltrated the group during the crusades, Da Vinci reshaped the group into the Eagles. The Bruces missed the reorganization, which had included the Henrys in the region renamed Virginia. The Bruces never survived the attacks in New York, and the survivors were assimilated into the United India company's agendas.

Tobias read through the information and rubbed his head. Under the circumstances, he might lose his friends at the former clinic. Pulling forward the thread of the conversation with Joe and Gabriella, Tobias decided to put Donna's and Eli's project under the radar. His knowledge of botanical medicine bonded him to Plymouth Plantation, a slave encampment. The pilgrims resisted the Moor's pills. The routes stemming from Iona severed the ties, freeing the inhabitants over time. He noticed how much work the world had to do to recover their vision from the illusionists. His father had made things simple. Like his walk on the mountain, even the reflections of the illumined ones could be used to find a path in the dark.

The Sons of Liberty fed the illusion of freedom. Nobody trusted them. Though overextended financially, Tobias enjoyed excellent health. He searched through his notes on Metatron's Cube. Having researched the topic during his undergraduate studies, Tobias reviewed the information on the pyramid civilizations.

His wife strolled in the room as he examined his drawings. Sitting down across from him, she relaxed. When Michelle saw his pictures, she remarked, "It's odd that three of the five aspects concern pyramids. Why not the Grand Canyon or the Himalayas?"

Tobias put his feet on the desk and stretched. "With the excepting of Singing Cave, these are all human-made structures created before the time of Christ."

"The humans needed the most help."

"The last aspect became active nine months before the Mayan calendar ended, which began the cycle."

"The ending constituted a birth," Michelle observed. "They figured that it would take 17,011 years to get pregnant."

Tobias laughed. "That's family planning." Then he abruptly changed the subject, "My father has been working as an undercover agent."

"What has he uncovered?" Michelle asked.

"His friends in the Pentagon support the MidEarth."

"There's more to the pyramids than slave labor, human sacrifice, and intergalactic wars."

"Tolkein only wrote about the period before the intergalactic wars. The pentagon derivatives from Metatron's Cube tell the story of the intergalactic wars and the period following it."

"Did we win?"

"17,011 years later." He shifted his position and lowered his feet to the floor. Sitting upright, he announced, "I need to let go of the clinic. The staff left the profession for jobs in insurance and pharmaceuticals." With a sigh, he took a deep breath, "My father told me."

"They made a choice, Tobias."

"In light of 17, 011 years, I'm keeping my freedom."

Michelle left the room to finish storing her midwifery gear. After putting his notes away, Tobias went to prepare dinner in the kitchen. When Michelle met him at the dinner table, he merely stared at his plate. He excused himself and went for a walk outdoors. The weeks passed and he dove into his work schedule without the usual enthusiasm. The insurance companies demanded a refund for his services, after losing him in their data bases. Another insurance company wanted him to see patients for only ten-minute visits. After settling the matter with several lengthy phone calls, Tobias decided to go to bed early that evening.

He recalled hearing an aunt tell him about a ship of immigrants from Germany. Hovering over the wooden craft from the 1800's, he watched the passengers collect rainwater with their clothes. The captain of the boat refused them water, so they stuck to their own devices. Half of the passengers died.

After a light sleep, Tobias awoke and rose from his bed. Sitting up, Michelle turned on the light. She blinked at him as he stepped into the legs of his trousers. "Did you have a nightmare about the United India company?"

"How did you know?" Tobias asked, before leaving the room for the kitchen.

In the dim light, he grabbed a glass and filled it with water. Staring out the window at the snowcapped peaks in the distance, he sipped the liquid. After witnessing how the insurance companies harassed both the physicians and clients, he dropped his own policy so that his enemies could not track his health. Keeping his good health under the radar, he found that he had more flexibility in business deals. There still remained a chance that he might work with Donna's project.

Michelle joined him downstairs. Without turning on any more lights, she brewed a cup of ginger tea. Her bathrobe tightly clad her figure as she steadied herself at the counter. She gulped, before remarking, "I dreamed about a buzzard circling Iron Mountain. My plans are to hid my connection, until it's safe to come out in the open."

Belonging to Diana, the goddess of the hunt and childbirth, the falcon had showed them how to reach the MidEarth. Tobias finished his drink and went back to bed, while Michelle prepared for the next birth. The next day, he returned to work and enjoyed a busy, productive day. Over time, some doctors from other clinics made offers. Tobias established a very powerful network, while maintaining his independence from the nightmarish United India company. He waited for the moment when he could resume working with Donna's project.

One day, Tobias received a call from Donna. She told him, "Princess Diana opposed Isabella's pursuit of Michael, but she arrived too late."

"That must be how she obtained his airships," he surmised.

"All was not lost," she said before quickly ending the call. "I must get back to my *chi gung* training. Tell me how's it going with the loss of the clinic?"

"There's still a chance that the others might return, but I've already accepted the loss."

"Enjoy your rest, Tobias. Bye."

Thirty minutes later, a colleague from another clinic called Tobias. "I want chart notes on all your patients."

"You are only entitled to the ones we share and you must get their approval," Tobias responded with a sense of betrayal. "Go get what you need from the electronic notes at the hospital. The receptionist there can help you."

The man hung up without further inquiry. Stunned by the his demands, Tobias wondered how many others were jeopardizing the health of their clients. He severed his relationship with this office.

In the evening, Michelle awoke startled. She rose from the bed and hurried to the kitchen. Underneath soft light, she recounted the nightmare to Tobias. He had stayed up late to do more research. With a gentle hug, Tobias comforted her. Having heard her dream, he promised, "I'm staying away from this outfit, even if they want to restart the clinic."

Chapter Thirteen

THE NEXT MORNING, Tobias found a signal from his father. In the middle of the front porch, he saw a pile of leaves with a piece of paper. The paper had been shaped in the form of an arrow. A small stone held the paper arrow in place on the leaves. Tobias checked with an intuitive for help in deciphering the message.

"He wants you to leave the car at house a few blocks away. His intelligence operations want an alert system on your vehicle for your protection," the reader said.

Tobias paid the reader and did as requested, after explaining the situation to Michelle. She supported his efforts, appearing surprised by the proximity of the safe house. The house harbored several agents in the area. Several days later, Tobias retrieved his vehicle from the same place where he left it. Whoever put the alarm system on his car, could enter the locked vehicle and drive it away without needing his keys. He had walked by the street on the previous day and seen it missing.

Within the week, he noticed a message flash across the LED screen. Without a second guess, he turned down the next street to avoid trouble. He tried another route home, but the message flashed again. Turning down another road, the message ceased for a few block and then reappeared. After a series of trials and errors, he eventually made it home.

"They wanted you to bypass an incident," the intuitive confirmed when Tobias called to check. "They arrested several people."

"I suppose that I am the bait."

"You're lucky. Other people are getting killed."

After ending the conversation, Tobias reviewed his notes on Las Vegas. Founded by an Armenian, the establishment became a haven for thugs depicted in the *Threepenny Opera*. Some people wanting a better life resorted to alternative medicine, whereas others chose the knife.

As another term for lawyer, a shark saw justice differently than those preying on a desert oasis. The genocide in Armenia wiped out Unani and nature-based medicine. The survivors brought their knives to California.

Like the jackal, a shark denoted a beast, one fulfilling a role in the natural scheme. Orin, the raptorgryph brought wealth down to earth. He glanced at the picture taken with Orin at Iron Mountain. The bird could peck out any Eye-in-the-Sky satellite. It remained for Tobias to disarm the airships, so that Orin's pointed beak and claws could get through. For the most part, the Eye-in-the-Sky airships lacked weaponry as their focus concerned espionage. If he provided a big enough distraction, Orin could destroy the eye.

Something on the heartless trade routes would do. So Tobias gathered five small to medium size mirrors and drove to Portland the next day. He placed them in various locations of the city, making a five-pointed pentagon in effect. Fifty yards separated each mirror. Then he drove tot he top of the hill at a nearby park. Overlooking the city, he waited to see if the alien satellite took the bait.

Thirty minutes later, an unmarked military chopper flew overhead. Orin's figure soared above it. The raptorgryph nose-dived, hitting the side of chopper. A cloud of smoke filled the sky and cloaked the city below in a rainstorm. Rays of sun filled the cracks in the vapor and a rainbow appeared where the chopper vanished. Tobias could make out Orin's silhouette in the golden light. The raptorgryph flew away as heavy drops of water splashed those on the ground. Tobias raced back to his car and turned up the heat. Halfway home, his clothes dried completely.

A warning message flashed on the LED screen as he neared his house. Turning down a dirt road, he waited a few minutes in a secluded area. The message returned and he backtracked. Instead of going home, he went to his former clinic. Vacated for several months, FOR-SALE signs hung in the windows. Parking in the abandoned lot, Tobias got out of his car and walked to a cafe, where he had once enjoyed an occasional lunch.

Entering the familiar place, Tobias listened to the sound of his shoes stepping on the painted cement floor. He approached the counter with minor hesitation and order a cup of hot chocolate.

"Where've you been?" the attendant greeted as he nodded over his pad to write down the order.

"Oh, just taking responsibility for my father's reality," he responded.

"Sounds like you are off to a fresh-start," the attendant remarked.

Moments later, Tobias nodded when he sipped his way through the whipped cream to the beverage. Grains of nutmeg dotted the white clouds layered over the dark, organic mixture. The young man raised his hand in a mock high five. In a low voice, he said, "Thanks, doc."

Tobias grinned and sat down at a seat by the window. Checking the news application on his cell phone, he learned that a large chopper had gone down off the Oregon Dunes. He glanced at the misty, gray skies and called Michelle.

"I might have to get a hotel room in town. The roads aren't safe for me to drive. An ounce of prevention is worth a pound of cure."

"I know, Tobias," she agreed. "You're a different man from your father. Stay in touch. I must run off to a birth soon."

While he waited in the cafe, Tobias called his buddies and gabbed. Late in the evening, he made another attempt to return home. This time no signal thwarted him. He found a note from Michelle in kitchen, saying that she had been called to a birth. Remaining at home for the next several days, he sensed the presence of his father's undercover organization. Safe and secure at home, he contentedly waited for his wife's return. Michelle spent over two days assisting with the labor until a colleague relieved her. She returned home and found Tobias studying in his office.

"My father sent a message to avoid Group 5," he mentioned.

"Aren't they the ones, who poisoned your aunt?"

"They work for the same outfit that contaminated the water at the family home in New Orleans."

Wiping a dry tear from his eye, Tobias deviated from the subject matter. He said ruefully, "Their sponsors funded Columbus and set up the Spanish Inquisition."

"I see," Michelle murmured. Bowing her head slightly, she looked at his arrangement of notes and swallowed hard.

"Isabella brought the Sicilian mob to Spain to secure her reign. Sicilians ran her military."

"This is the ruler, who pursued the archangel Michael?"

"His archenemy. She died in Medina, Spain. Her father had an alliance with the Moors. Henry VIII had an alliance with Medina, Spain. He married Isabella's younger sister."

"I suppose that got him started."

"Apparently, he started killing his wives afterwards."

"I see," Michelle repeated. She rose from her chair and headed for the kitchen. "Would you like a cup of elderberry flower tea?"

Returning with the brew, she handed a cup to Tobias. He told her, "Isabella descended from the Franks in Italy. They would have been under Salish law."

Savoring her tea, Michelle reflected on his words for a moment. "It appears that Gilgamesh's ancestors pursued the angels clear into the Spanish Inquisition."

"And the concentration camps of World War II."

Michelle quieted as Tobias continued, "From the looks of things, the gapers continue to compete with nature-based medicine."

"They have an alien agenda," Michelle surmised. "They made the Spanish Inquisition look like a religious war."

"They've had practice," Tobias observed.

"Nothing left to do, but ascend, Tobias," Michelle told him as she passed the threshold into the hallway.

"Where?" he asked after she left.

"High Sierras," she stated loudly from the other room.

Remaining seated, Tobias looked at the list of botanicals found in the High Sierras. They all vibrated at a higher frequency. Muir dubbed the mountains as the range of light. Excited by the prospect of heaven on earth, Tobias gathered his notes to confer with Michelle further on the expedition.

Mixing some flour and eggs together in a large bowl, Michelle armed a long wooden spoon in circles as she glanced at Tobias. "I know," she said. "Iron Mountain is called iron because it survived plate tectonics. The High Sierras operate at a higher frequency."

"Some of the mountains are called Crystal."

"Just like Crystal Mountain in the Cascades. The town of Paradise is at the base of Mount Rainer."

"Not on top," Tobias observed. "The Native Americans considered the flatlands around Mount Saint Helens as paradise, according to the notes. It must have been phenomenal in their time."

"Sierras is a Spanish name, Tobias. Isabella's company would have been aware of the extraterrestrial activity at the higher elevations."

"They left the area untouched."

"They wanted the pyramids and Seven Cities of Gold."

"Like Iron Mountain, the High Sierras have protection from nephilim. Occultists have yet to unlock its secrets."

"I kno-o-ow," Michelle said, rigorously stirring the mixture in the bowl.

"We know its secrets," Tobias said. "Its a runway strip."

"The Sequoias grow tall in the afterglow."

"The exhaust from these airships nourish the region."

"That's advanced."

"The Pantagons thrived on the stuff."

"Bottle it, Tobias."

"I don't want to be a giant, Michelle. I would look too odd compared to the company I keep. Besides, it is how the Titans got started. Sniffing too much ether. The only one that supported the earth in the end, was Atlas."

"Under the circumstances, his Atlantis might not have been such a good idea."

"I agree."

Chapter Fourteen

Their discussion continued as Tobias and Michelle considered the options. "We must go back to how the archangel Michael lost his terrible swift sword. The people orchestrating the Civil War took it. Abraham Linkhorn's (Lincoln) first wife tried to retrieve it." Tobias paused for a moment and stared outside. The snowcapped Cascades loomed in the distance. "Now how are we going to get back Michael's sword?" Tobias questioned.

"Keep working with the angels, Tobias," Michelle answered as she rose to leave the room. "Forgiveness is another path."

In the afternoon, Tobias saw patients where he worked part-time. Arriving several hours early, he organized his office in the back. A lawyer entered the lobby and ushered the receptionist and acupuncturist into another room. Hurrying down the hall, she failed to notice Tobias's presence in the clinic. She spoke in a loud, courtroom voice that pounded fear into the walls of the building. The physician running the clinic had the day off. Tobias wondered whether he knew that a lawyer had arrived to question the staff. The lawyer related a lawsuit concerning the demise of former patient to an allergy attack. The clinic had been named in the lawsuit.

Waiting for his client's arrival, Tobias overheard the lawyer continually repeat to the staff, "They want a lot of money."

The receptionist related her story in a choked voice. Tobias wondered about the legality of her testimony and the lawyer's scruples in the investigation. It appeared that she represented the other side, though the insurance company had sent her. As Tobias saw through the ruse, the image of a fiery red sword appeared in midair. The lawyer ended the interview and marched out of the clinic, armed with self-righteousness.

Tobias met his client as the receptionist dried her tears at the front desk. The acupuncturist hid in office with the door shut. After he finished his shift, Tobias returned home. The image of the blazing sword filled the atmosphere, affecting his feelings about case.

He met Michelle reviewing her notes. Seated at the dining table, she studied the latest information on B12 injections. Tobias stood beside her and stared at the assortment of magazine and journals.

"The clinic's chief officer handed me Michael's sword today," he stated.

"What happened?"

"The doctor is a latin from the Southwest with a German name," Tobias said. "I know the area and I can only guess about the past abuse. He's being set up in a lawsuit, one that occurred before I joined. His name means "knife." Under the circumstances, his approach seems reasonable. He underestimated the Asian mother's dislike for her daughter."

"They have a tradition of murdering their female progeny."

"They would do it to make themselves look good, especially in a foreign country."

"Time to get into that other clinic," Michelle observed. "Stay clear of this situation."

"Michael's sword cuts right through it and releases the intrigue. It is not black and white, otherwise."

"Let his truth win out. Grab the sword and run, Tobias. Take the clients that the clinic doesn't want, and go to the new one."

"The owner wouldn't tolerate this nonsense. She did *feng-shui*, according to the five elements. I recognized the work of her consultant. We hired the same one to do our home."

"There's synchronicity."

For several months, Tobias worked at the clinic with the five-element *feng-shui*. He continued his research as a defense against biased lawyers and his mother's organization. There remained a chance that his mother might kill him, like her younger sibling. His investigation led him to submit a paper on homeopathy.

"The only ones interested in scientifically validating homeopathy are the Russians," he told Michelle as they dined in the kitchen one morning. "The representative at the Defense Language Institute in Carmel, California collaborated with the head of research at the Naturopathic college."

"I'll support you," Michelle offered. "I have some extra funds. Go check it out."

"He says that the Russians want to use the science to obtain more funding from the communists."

"We could use that here," Michelle commented as she cleared her place.

In winter, Tobias left for the conference in Russia. He watched a young family from eastern Washington board the plane. Dressed in the traditional folk-style costume, the couple separated to fulfill gender-specific roles concerning the management of their large brood of small children. The rest of the passengers glumly braced in their reclined chairs for the long flight across the Arctic Circle.

Triggered by the casual site of apparently privileged Americans in Russia, Tobias began sobbing uncontrollably. The patriarch of the segregated family came over to comfort him by asking questions. Tobias learned that the patriarch's grandfather had been an Alaskan fisherman, who decided to stay in the United States after a line divided the Bering Strait. Keeping connected with the fatherland, he operated a successful construction business in the drier part of Washington State. His calm, confident manner reassured Tobias with its different perspective. Tobias dried his tears and explained that he was just a Naturopathic physician pursuing science, even if it took him to Moscow during December. Satisfied with Tobias's answer, the man moved back to his chair away from the family mayhem.

Tobias drifted into a semiconscious state and dozed. The next day, he awoke as the pilot announced that they had reached the Arctic Circle. Passengers rose and opened the shades on the windows.

The glare of the sun crystalized over the icy landscaper filled the cab-in. As a movie about an overgrown elf from New York played on the screens, Tobias closed his eyes. Under the intense white light, he could not find any darkness. A woman dressed in blue sat near the window, several seats over on the row. She smiled and nodded at him. He recalled a scene from the move *White Nights*, where a Russian defector reunites with a former lover in Saint Petersburg. Barely escaping the second time around, he opens his eyes to the light at the top of the world. In his mind, Tobias stood next to the injured ballet star. Never leaving the aisle, Tobias distanced himself from the other passengers, who sometimes tested him to determine whether he understood Russian.

Tobias awoke fully from his dream, after it dawned on him that it was too late to turn back. Reconciling his idealized notions of science to his greedy reach above the clouds, he glanced at the passengers in the row and determined that the lady in blue had been a mirage. Not only that, he had already committed himself to the wrong direction.

When he returned home, he told Michelle, "The scientists at the conference said, 'I was brave.'"

"What else?"

"Well, there is no right to assembly. Many of the scientists locked away in the university suites own flats in New York."

"Interesting," Michelle murmured. "Yet, others have the freedom to swim underwater with their newborns. Mothers go to the Caspian Sea for this."

"Red Square keeps Lenin's Eye-in-the-Sky mausoleum across from the orthodox church with the turnip-shaped roof. A physician, who does acupuncture for the cosmonauts, took me there. After two steps inside the place, we both freaked and decided not to spend our money on getting a ticket."

"I heard that the guy who built the structure went crazy."

"That's what the scientist whispered to me as we raced out. It never ended. If I worked behind solid brick walls almost twenty-five yards high, I'd go crazy too."

"Do think there are any trees in the Kremlin?"

"No, they don't do trees in Moscow. Probably no Druids, either."

"The lawyer investigating the last clinic worked for Kronos. Like a communist, she wanted to redistribute the money earned by hard-workers."

"Sorta like the KGB, and other orthodox-internet providers," Michelle said softly. "I really don't like sharing my conversations with everyone."

"After another scientist pointed out the masonry in Red Square, the passengers on the return plane puzzled over the resemblance to the United States dollar. Apparently Russia and India are on the same banking wavelength."

"Catherine the Great fought to trade with those on the spice route. Her sponsors planned a takeover here, prior to the American Revolution. The Romanovs reversed the trend and support-ed President Lincoln against the Catherine's sponsors."

"Medicine became an issue. Orthodoxy failed to heal the Romanov bloodline."

"You can see why the czar and his families defected."

"Isabella's Columbus company came after them."

"Corporations never die. The United States made sure of it."

"It all goes back to that golden bull worshipped under Solomon's Temple."

"An engineer from MIT told us that construction hasn't changed much since the Roman Empire, who probably looked to Solomon' Temple for designs."

"Orthodoxy is about never being able to think outside the box."

"Others, like the Druids preferred shataquahs, which are round like a Round Table."

"You can see the conflict between the square peg and the round hole."

"Which brings us back to gender-cide."

"Masons take responsibility for that tradition, which began with the infestation of the Tree of Life."

"Like ants, they run the military and have crawled all over Korea."

"My father never became an occultist. He never cared for orthodoxy, preferring the tactics of the Native Americans."

Chapter Fifteen

Tune Reference: *Prayer for the Four Directions*

----David and Steve Gordon

INTENDING TO PURIFY after his trip to Russia, Tobias gathered with his friends at a Native American ceremony. Every Sunday morning the group convened to *Call in the Four Directions*, realigning with the four compass directions of the earth in a sacred celebration. Tobias sat down with the others as the chanting and drumming began. A leader lit a peace pipe and passed it around those assembled on the floor of a conference room.

When his turn to speak arrived, Tobias talked about his findings in Moscow. He told them about the disturbances to the electromagnetic field of the planet due to the masonry in Red Square. "Their medicine exploits the earth's spirit. Anyone who says anything gets destroyed. My research indicates that their soldiers killed Sacagawea, after murdering Meriwether Lewis. The Salish opposed this group many, many years ago. They continue to utter one of the world's primary languages as a family. They recaptured the medicine spirit around Smoking Mountain or Louwala-Clough, which a British officer recorded as Mount Saint Helens during the creation of the French Republic."

Tobias took a few puffs on the peace pipe and passed it on. The Native American next to him elaborated, "The Salish called the river around Smoking Mountain *Tawallitch*, or Cowlitz. It means 'capturing the medicine spirit.' The medicine of Gilagamesh's ancestors lacks spirit. We escaped and the Yeti took us to the Sasquatch here. The Iroquois Confederacy changed to bring in the Five Nations to counter the Pentarch. They renounced Salish Law and brought in women to help lead, as the European natives did after Atlantis."

Passing on the peace pipe, the young man raised his hand to indicated that he had more to relate. "We separated with help from the activity on the High Sierras. Our former relations could not pursue us when we travelled those realms."

The pipe made its way around the circle and an elder concluded the sacred ceremony. Afterwards, Tobias lingered and sipped green tea. Several elders from the group approached him. One said, "There's still a chance that the dark side will take over the region."

Tobias stared at him and replied, "Years ago, the jackal was pursued by the same outfit that had renamed Louwala-Clough. In 2006, one of their agents wrote about the connection between this region and Hades's operation. Hades remains as one of the chiefs of the Salish tribes east of the Himalayas."

Taking a deep breath, Tobias waved a feather in the air. The elder told him, "Yes, we gifted you with that goose feather years ago. I remember."

"The feather lifted me to the next level of understanding," Tobias mentioned. "Now that I understand the flight across the Bering Strait, I can move forward in other realms without stirring up trouble."

"Here's a white feather for you, Tobias," a woman announced as she handed him the feather with a red ribbon tied around the stem. "We see you grieving the loss of the Dixie dollar and the Anasazi in the four corners of Utah, New Mexico, Colorado, and Arizona."

After Napoleon claimed the French Revolution, the Southwest natives traded Dixie currency with the French in New Orleans. This prevented Napoleon from seizing the trade routes, which had been established by the Anasazi to construct the Seven Cities of Cibola. Before Isabella's troops landed in the Southwest, the cities were placed in another dimension for hiding precious minerals. Unlike the Spanish, the Apaches knew how to use time to their advantage.

"Focus on what you have left, Tobias," the elder said as he departed from the gathering.

Tobias left the scene and drove home to Michelle. Ruefully shaking her head as she looked down at the kitchen counter, she told him, "Isabella's minions threaten midwifery. I need your help, Tobias."

"Isabella worshipped the goddesses of fate. The truth of the matter is that nobody rules life and death, not even Zeus's daughters, Lachesis, Atropa, or Clotho."

"Not even the insurance companies of the Roman Empire."

"CPH and Associates claim that Genoa became the first to offer maritime insurance, but no policy was recorded for Columbus. Being a local, they apparently understood the risk. A hundred years after his undertaking, Lloyds of London took control of the shipping and demanded insurance." Taking a deep breath, Tobias added, "London's bank sat on top of fallen Roman temple."

"I see," Michelle answered. "The insurance in this country is owned by patriots of the United India company."

"Not only do they answer to Lloyds, they work with Isabella's Sicilian armies to control the outcomes, like the fates. Stay away from the fates and you'll be okay. Your destiny lies with the four directions, which includes the celestial realm."

Placing his cup down on the counter, he cocked his head as he listened to the birds chattering around the outdoor feeder. "In the native culture, only a wise owl can make a call on death. They sing songs like *I Heard the Owl Call My Name*. The Pacific Northwest natives find wisdom in the undertaking, rather than chaos." Tobias added on another note, "We used to sing it at mass in Texas, unaware that the tradition came from the Northwest. Like clamshells, good music gets traded quickly. I don't know about the copyright law on this one."

Leaving the room, Tobias told her, "Back in a moment, Michelle. I have a crow feather for you."

Within fifteen minutes, Tobias returned to Michelle with a large, black feather. As he gave the feather, he explained, "My aunt Carol told me about how women bragged about the crows, which came to their yards. They would say *my crow is blacker than your crow*."

Michelle laughed, waving her jet black feather in the air. "Thanks for the gift, Tobias. These days all nurturers need another set of arms."

"It will help you evolve without being noticed."

"There's still a chance that I might be able to keep midwifery going. I really enjoy bringing in new life."

Smiling at her statement, Tobias put his arm around her. Then he left to meet Native Americans at the conference room on the other side of town. This time, they wanted to discuss their own safety in dealing with the challenges of a changing environment.

"We have Pakistan operating in our vicinity," one elder observed. "The British serve them. If we don't sidestep this conflict of interest, we will get caught in the fray."

"Let's not repeat ten thousand years of mistakes," another elder voiced to the seated crowd. "We'll give them the casinos."

"That'll keep us out of it. Let's not bring the war to this conti-nent."

The assembly ratified the measure by a wide margin. They set up provisions for returning the casinos to the Brahmins and snake-wor-shippers. Afterwards, Tobias went home and brought the news to Michelle.

"The natives didn't want their children to have a fear-based edu-cation," Tobias remarked.

"That just leaves mass immunizations," Michelle commented as she poured hot chocolate into his mug. Savoring her concoction, she informed him, "I am trading in the midwifery business for botanical medicine."

Tobias put his cup on the counter with a subtle thud. In a soft voice, he uttered, "Whew!"

Michelle turned and stared at him.

Meeting her gaze, Tobias offered, "After reaching the Arctic Circle, I learned my lesson about science."

"That the earth is truly round?" she questioned with a slight smirk.

Tobias chuckled lightly. Taking a sip from his mug, he swallowed hard. "No. It's too late to teach ecocentric narcissists that the planet revolves around the sun. Never try to rescue a drowning person; they'll pull you in."

"In other words, treat only those who come to the clinic. No passengers allowed."

"Birth is a transition. Women will have to go back to delivering on their own or be tortured by the United India company. It is Salish Law. I didn't understand the science until I was halfway around the world."

"They can always go to school and get a midwifery degree for birthing their own babes."

"That would be prudent."

"We are not Gauds."

"Yes, that bloodline is falling apart. We cannot keep them from their dramas and self-destruction."

"Obviously, with Hades's daughter in our own backyard."

"The agent for the United India company entitled her *The Afghan*."

"These are the same people who would turn a president born in a log cabin into an icon, after serving him to Rome on a dish."

Chapter Sixteen

~1198 AD. Spain

SYLVAN'S TRADE EXPANDED with the Eleanor's placement of the Merry men and women near the Pyrenees. Eight years later, he journeyed to Spain to meet with several new vendors, establishing an alternative trade route for Henry II. Bypassing the violence of the crusades, Henry's group in Medina, Spain networked with the *Aws* in Medina, Arabia. Henry II sidestepped the descendants of the prophet, and avoided confrontations with his sons.

As the sons of Vlad the Impaler kept the family in business, the first two generations adopted their deceased father's name to create the impression of immortality. This inspired a unique sect within the Arab population to unite as one. They used this unification as an excuse to murder dissidents, rape, and steal property. Everyone had to became a company man, fighting a religious war. Based on the Roman model of a city-state, the company chose to believe in one Gaud, at the expense of all the others. However, others saw through the facade carved in stone and prayed for a more enlightened world. Instead of trying to restore the Garden of Eden, they opted for a more colorful version, complete with rainbow.

Sylvan provided refuge to those fleeing Arabia for the settlement in the Pyrenees. Meeting a physician amongst the group head west, he organized a group of warriors to promote the practice. He recognized the medicine coming from the walls of Iona and advised Henry II on the subject.

"The Arabs are bringing us our own medicine," he told Henry II while he vacationed with Eleanor at their winter castle.

"It's the least that they could do, after running us over," Henry II commented. "It's karma. Now they are on the run."

"We need to keep it away from the Moors, who set up the crucifixions in Jerusalem."

"One day the witch doctors will create a place without the Jeru and simply call it Salem."

The Jerus, as the descendants of the archangel Michael through the line of priests called Melchezidiak, bestowed blessings on all of Abraham's descendants, including Ishmael's family of Arabs. For this reason, the chariots of the Roman Empire decided to run right over Jerusalem and put down their spirit. Witch doctors from Africa paid for the chariots, which turned the tide against the angels. Unleashing the demons from Africa resulted in a fury of slander hurled at the Israelites as well as the Ishmaelites. Boundaries became diffuse, as the distinction between black and white blurred. A massive witch hunt developed as a result of the inquisition, which killed those questioning the big picture.

"We need to stave off the inquisition heading this way, before Arabia and the Holy Roman Empire decide to question each other."

"I suggest seeking exile," Sylvan offered. "It is one way to quit sitting on a fence, which is about to be destroyed."

"Robin Hood has left us."

"Murdered by his own hoods. None of them want to replace him."

"They made it rough for everyone, including themselves."

"In the end, the addicts provided no advantage. They became difficult to manage," Henry II commented, ruefully shaking his head over the plight. "There's still a chance that Marie might be killed. If the Roman legions succeed, then we loose everything."

"We must keep Champagne. I will bring this physician to France. He can help deal with the priory next door."

"Oh yes, the one with the black rose," he said, wiping away a tear that had escaped from his eye. Atlantean dark wizards modified local flora to create genetic signatures. "They left their flower with Scholastique's corpse."

"Eleanor can provide support from Aquitaine," Sylvan said with a sigh. "She also is vulnerable, like her daughter, Marie."

"How is Rousseau handling Avalon?"

"They intend to restore it in Connecticut."

"Great, my relations are resettling in the region near the First Nations. The natives carry on the traditions of the Golden Poppy there. The Curtmantles have leased tracts of land west of the portal."

After Norman's conquest, Henry's family relocated in Scotland. The elders wore short jackets, known as curtmantles. Known by the name of their jacket, the organization gained a reputation for riding fast horses. Wearing a short jacket, the members enjoyed greater speed due to less weight on the horse. A distant relation, Robert Curthose, died in the London Tower as result of innovative fashion threatening Roman designs.

"They can carry the traditions of Iona as well," Sylvan observed.

Henry II stepped silently toward Sylva, standing only an inch shorter than Henry. The forest diet favored his rapid, balanced growth. "I have a favor to ask."

"Let me guess," he said eyeing Henry carefully. "You want me to work with the physician and teach his kinsfolk to ride as fast as the Curtmantles."

"That's my answer."

"That's what we'll call them. Our *Answrs* to the Byzantine and Sassanid Empires."

"I promise not to look a gift-horse in the mouth. Who cares where they came from. Put them to work."

"More is not better."

"Try to tell the Moors that. Their African doctors have bewitched them into taking over everything."

"Especially us."

"Let's get started before they start putting bulls in the Spanish coliseums."

"They find that it is less expensive than funding chariots and drivers."

"Speaking of chariots, you'll need to speak to the limeys to get proper horses for your Arabian knights."

The pyramid civilization called Potbelly Hill, had been avoided by the Roman Emperor, King Antiochus. He placed seafaring barbarians from western Africa to create lines of defense. Called Limes Arabicus, the displaced sailors failed to ever mount the horses roaming the Goblecki Tepe and Gyan Tepe. Ancestors of the physician came from this region, near the birthplace of Abraham. His connections could help bring the horses to Spain.

Sylvan left Henry II and met with the physician. Sitting down on the edge of his cot, he gazed at the dirt floor of the tent. He looked with Sylvan with tears in his eyes. "This is a war which we will loose," he said shaking his head.

Sylvan sat down on a nearby cushion. "Both Henry and I agree that we cannot survive the threats here."

"The Husain clan possess the celestial knowledge."

"Are they the escapees from Goblecki Tepe?"

"They never escaped."

Sylvan rose from the curtain and went outside for a breath of fresh air. He walked past two tents and called to the gypsy reader inside the third tent. Immediately responding, she drew back the veil concealing the entrance and ushered him to a seat near a small table.

"I know about your dealing with Henry II and the refugees." Without further hesitation, she told Sylvan about Crierwy's mission with the scrolls taken from a temple in the desert. Crierwy had hid the scrolls in caves tended by the Bedouins. The Roman Empire tortured them into submission and the sect lost their connection with the documents in the caves. The illusionists seized other libraries as they searched the area for the original site, the one torched by Welsh dragons. These scrolls mentioned an intergalactic pentagon.

"We can't win until we restore the intergalactic pentagon in some form on the planet," Sylvan surmised after listening to her story.

"Otherwise the planet is programmed to self-destruct. Henry II doesn't know this."

"Leprechauns told me about a cave in the Himalaya Mountains, which sings before major earth changes."

"Those who escape the pyramid civilizations often see rainbows. Ask the physician whether he knows about Singing Cave."

Sylvan left and returned to the gypsy. Shaking his head, he stared at the dirt floor and told her that the physician had not heard of the Singing Cave.

"Too bad," she responded. "The descendants of Abraham are controlled by those exploiting the Himalayan poppy, which envelopes the unsuspecting in illusion. Monks in the area take care of Singing Cave, rather than cultivate the golden poppy."

"The pentagon must reflect this in some way," Sylvan rejoined.

"It is already carved in Metatron's cubes. The sands for healing can be found with the Apaches. These Toltecs survived an air attack on their pyramid and seeded a new nation. Now the Gulf coast serves as Spain's next target."

"It is like the Lemurians, who survived to seed the Druids or the Atlanteans survivors emerging as the Celts."

"Let these *Answrs* mesh back into their people. They aren't fighting an air attack; they fight their own brother."

Recalling the ancient feud between Cain and Abel, Sylvan told her, "You're right. That explains the lack of inspiration. It is a setup for failure."

"Occultists from Spain have already infiltrated Avalon. They cloud the mysteries with their own perversions."

"What mysteries?" Sylvan asked.

"There are none. It's another illusion."

The physician entered the gypsy's tent unannounced. "Please forgive the intrusion. I overheard and decided to simplify matters by joining the discussion."

"Tell us where we can find Husain," the gypsy demanded.

"He's in the campground, several tents down the row. Follow me."

Stepping outside, fresh breeze emanating from the top of the nearby hillside pushed Sylvan in the same direction where the physician pointed. Without a knock or greeting, they entered the tent and found Husain comfortably reclined on a bed of cushions. "Hurry inside before the Roman legions attack. I sensed your arrival." Handing several rolls of papyrus to Sylvan, he offered, "Here are the designs for a pentagon on this planet."

Sylvan studied the material with the gypsy looking over his shoulder. Afterwards, he told everyone around him, "Let's break camp and beat the Roman chariots."

Taking the scrolls with him, he went immediately to the camp director, "We are helping a prisoner escape his foes. Disguise the group as a caravan bound for a performance at Aquitaine. We must get out of Spain, before they kill us all."

Chapter Seventeen

THE CAMP QUICKLY reorganized into a caravan and left Spain without a trace. The rear guard erased any markings from footprints, wheels, or horse's hooves. Two day later, they unloaded the barges carrying them to France. Sylvan continued his trade along the route as he taught the Arabian knights the basics about living lightly on the terrain. This enabled quick escapes and kept the horses free from extended duress. The less they engaged this enemy, the better.

Riding his horse along the beach and surveying the exodus, Sylvan paused and remarked to an officer standing near, "The troops are discouraged and so am I." Then without a further comment, he galloped away to help a couple from Medina keep their two small boys from falling in the river."

After bringing the family to the shore, he waited for the rest to cross safely. He glanced longingly at the nearby woods. With a shrug and a sigh, he tighten his grip on his reins before turning around to lead the caravan to the village outside of Aquitaine. Reaching their destination several days later, they set up a festive camp.

Eleanor arrived on horseback the next day to meet her latest group of troubadours and meet with Sylvan. "So you decided against a foray into King Antiochus's domain."

"Later," Sylvan replied as he tended chores. "We found plenty of horses after we razed a nearby Moorish town. It was for practice."

"Great. Now you are in my court," Eleanor told him as she allowed her horse to feed on some hay scattered on the ground.

Sylvan looked up at her. He placed his toolkit on a bench and walked over to pat the nose on her steed. "I do not intend to die satisfying Henry's greed. He underestimates the limeys and the karma of Cain versus Abel. Rome's Arabs already pursue the warriors that he asked me to equip with horses. Henry left me with a camp of hopeless cases."

Pulling away from him. Eleanor turned and said, "I am at odds with Henry II. My sons are pursuing him. He will not bother us, so let the entertainment begin."

Sylvan resumed his work before instructing the physician how to train the knights in his absence. Carrying his wares further north, he journeyed to the Alemanni's encampment hidden in the forests. A woman emerged from one of the huts as he tied his horse to a post.

"I need your intervention," he told her. "I heard about you from the refugees in Medina. You're a Queen from Angles, Germany."

"True, but you mustn't tell Eleanor or Henry II. I intend no harm, nor do I want their kingdoms."

For several days, Sylvan stayed alone with the woman called Angie. She told him about the Templar knights invading Germany from Jerusalem. "They pledged allegiance to the Germaine, the same Atlantean wizard who had destroyed King Arthur's Court. First, they kill the herbalists and midwives, then they replace the medicine from Iona with a Vedhic version imported from the Serpentine's nests in the Himalayas."

Deciding to investigate the local base associated with Avalon, he followed her to a circle of women congregated in a town five miles away. Imitating the traditions of the Teutonic knights from the lower chambers of Solomon's temple, the horn-nosed women cackled and threw animal parts into a boiling pot hanging over the campfire. Sylvan gasped and his friend ran with him back to the nearest river. Safe from the sensitivities of the fallen angles, Sylvan and Angie swam in the water for refreshment.

The sound of horses hooves echoed through the forest, drowning out the melodious rush of the current racing downstream. The couple hurried out of the water and hid behind the dense brush along the beach. Hordes of hooded men raced toward the witches' cauldron. Sylvan and Angie mounted their steeds and headed back to Alemanni base. The anguished screams of both men and women pierced the air. They reached the Alemanni lingering on the edge of the woods by midmorning.

"We heard the commotion and decided to check on it," one man explained as he helped Angie find food for the horses. "Remnants of Robin's hoods called upon the witches. We left this battle for the sharif."

"Sheriff?" Angie questioned.

"Henry's son, John has brought sharifs from the wizards surrounding Potbelly Hill to contain Rome's citizens, or *pagi*. These illusionists intend to erase real knowledge with violence. Soon everyone will entertain the notion that Avalon belongs to witches."

Together, they made their way back to the base as they discussed the deception darkening the forests. Area wood nymphs communicated their concerns about the environmental poisoning. Sylvan stopped short of the hut. Kissing Angie on the cheek, he promised, "It's time to resurrect Robin Hood and his group of Merry Men. We will take back our forest."

Before anyone could disagree, Sylvan mounted his horse and fled back to Aquitaine for the choir escapees from England. A few days later, they met in a spare room inside Eleanor's castle. Eleanor listened from a peephole in the next room, in case roaming inquisitors came an asked her whether she had been present. Refusing to lie, she manipulated circumstances to ease her conscience and avoid potential torture from warlocks gifted with remote sensing capabilities. At one point during the discussion, she aired her sentiment in a loud monologue, so that everyone could hear.

"Kill the Socialists from the basement of Solomon's Temple!" she cried in a voice, befitting the best of her actors. "Ever since the Temple occultists sacrificed the Brahmin artist, we've had nothing but cookie-cutters and assembly-line medicine. Where are my artists?"

Those in the next room heartily clapped and raised goblets of mead in salutation.

Encouraged by the fanfare, Eleanor continued to shout, "Where are my scientists? All we have now are vengeance-based brews that consume the passions of roving maniacs."

"Cheers!" the merry bunched yelled in chorus. Adding softly, someone said, "Let's not get carried away. The forest awaits Sylvan's return!"

As if by cue, the merriment dashed out of the castle and was never seen or heard from again. Sylvan gave up his blue tunic for a green one. Refusing to wear tights, he laced up his leggings and put a robin's feather in his hat.

"What a change!" Angie exclaimed when she checked out his new image.

A low rumble erupted from a region several miles north. His merry group cried, "Robin, it's time to fly!"

Sylvan kissed her good-bye.

"Wait, Robin. Where are you going?"

He smiled at her. Turning to the group racing for their props and weapons, he replied, "We're rob-bin' hoods."

"What? You intend to steal from thieves?"

"Somebody had got to save them from the witches' cauldrons. We haven't put out their fires yet."

"What?"

"We save forests; we save men; we keep cold women cold."

"It's a service!" a merry person hollered.

"It's a calling!" another merry warrior said with glee.

"It beats the owls calling my name," Sylvan explained with a slight shrug. He ran from Angie to join his former choir. Glancing over his shoulder, he asked Angie, "Will you meet me at the river in an hour. Bring a picnic for two. I'll go find some wine. Love, you!"

"Wait, don't you have insurance?"

"For my life or my health?"

"Both."

"What's insurance?"

"C'mon, Sylvan," someone merrily chided. "Let's go rob some hoods. Insurance is where you pay a Teutonic knight from the basement of the temple in Jerusalem to protect you from the snake-worshippers."

"Are the owls part of this?"

"Only the ones on the Gaud's coins. The forest owls are wiser."

"No," Sylvan told Angie. "But maybe we can pay the Teutonic knights to protect us from the snake worshippers."

"The Phoenicians would be upset."

"How do you spell that?"

"Phonetically or upset?"

"Upset. They rely on the pyramid or temple scheme for their trades."

When the witch doctors began working with the Moors, they adopted the insurance program to fit their own agendas. Those threatening the slave trade became targets of the Sicilians protecting insurance programs, which sometimes were only thinly-veiled genocide programs. Those cultures remaining free from such institutions became plagued by the mob control.

To avoid the influx of Sicilians controlling movement in the area, Sylvan and his merry group moved to Lyons. The monastery there served the vital interests of the trade with Iona. Offering protection in exchange for choir practice, they ensured their merry way. Sylvan left the Alemanni to their own protective devices. Coming out of the shadows, Sylvan forced many of the region's hidden enemies into the open. Unable to take advantage of the fear and the dark, the exposure gave the public greater clarity and the criminals vanished. The local populace believed that Robin Hood remained alive.

Angie continued to hide in the forests surrounding the Alemanni. In the presence of strong men, the Sicilian network failed. Sylvan often rendezvous with her at various locations along the river. Working with Angie, the Lyon trade route escaped notice of the Sicilians. The Alemanni could bring their wares to Angie for trade. Friars joined the commerce, circulating their bread, wine, and cheese for wild game and tapestries to attract congregations.

After losing the connection with Eleanor and Henry II, Sylvan watched the sharifs gain power over more area. He let go of his Arabian knights as the sharifs came. They got caught in Cain versus Abel dynamics and destroyed one another. The surviving Arabian nights returned to Jerusalem to menace their brothers who worshipped the temple, instead of them.

Meanwhile, Sylvan continued to gather nuts. The squirrels buried some of their reserves and seeded more trees for nuts, which Sylvan collected. Many of the trade routes became lined with trees as the result of Sylvan's wanderings and the squirrel's offerings. In this manner, he achieved his lifelong goal in protecting trees and saving the planet with the help of Angie.

BIBLIOGRAPHY

Andrews, Ted. *Animal Speak*. St. Paul, Minnesota: Lewellyn Publications, 1993.